Praise for Eve Vaughn's *Stranded*

"*Stranded* is all about staying alive. ...*Stranded* is jam-packed with red hot sex and emotions enough to elevate your blood pressure. This is a fantastic story that I enjoyed a great deal."

~ *Rosemary, Joyfully Reviewed*

4.5 Hearts, Sensuality rating: Explicit "I loved how the author took such a realistic view to the pitfalls of being stranded on a deserted island. Their survival wasn't sugar coated and that made the romance all the more realistic. ...Definitely they are some of the strong people who has made lemonade out of the lemons they were served!"

~ *Lisa Freeman, The Romance Studio*

Look for these titles by
Eve Vaughn

Now Available:

The Life and Loves of April Johnson
A Night to Remember
The Reinvention of Chastity

Stranded

Eve Vaughn

A SAMHAIN PUBLISHING, LTD. publication.

Samhain Publishing, Ltd.
577 Mulberry Street, Suite 1520
Macon, GA 31201
www.samhainpublishing.com

Stranded
Copyright © 2008 by Eve Vaughn
Print ISBN: 978-1-59998-810-8
Digital ISBN: 1-59998-664-7

Editing by Angela James
Cover by Scott Carpenter

First Samhain Publishing, Ltd. electronic publication: August 2007
First Samhain Publishing, Ltd. print publication: June 2008

Dedication

To my girls: Nic, Ro, and Shar. Thanks for the support and laughter, ladies.

Chapter One

"Have you any idea the embarrassment you've caused this family, young lady?"

India stared at the floor, unable to meet her father's intense scrutiny.

"Your father is speaking, the least you can do is look at us when we're addressing you," Leila Powers scolded.

India lifted her head, still not catching either parent's gaze. "What do you expect me to say?"

Her father huffed in his annoyance. "An explanation would be a start. What were you thinking to make a scene like that—in front of all those people no less? Haven't we taught you better than that?"

Wrapping her arms around herself, India stood and walked over to the window. The fierceness of their stares burned a hole in her back. "Everything there is to say was said at the restaurant. Steven and I are through. I can't marry him."

"Are you out of your ever lovin' mind? He's a Cartwright! Do you know how connected his family is? Not to mention their money. What possible reason could you have for rejecting and humiliating a fine young man like that—and us?" Her mother's voice had grown progressively louder with each word spoken.

India was fast losing her temper. She'd called off her engagement tonight and all her parents could think about was themselves. Any second now they'd mention Jack.

"Jack would never act the way you did tonight. I'm very disappointed in you, India." Her father acted as if she'd just committed murder.

Tears swam in her eyes and she let her arms fall to her sides, fists clenched. "I've always been a disappointment to you two, so what else is new?"

Trevor Powers gripped her shoulder and turned India around to face him. "Don't sass me, girl."

She pulled out of his hold. "Do you really want to know why I called off the engagement? Because I caught your precious idol in bed with another woman!" she screamed her anger.

Her father recoiled as if he'd been hit.

"I guess Steven isn't as perfect as you guys think he is," India muttered.

India's mother joined them, and patted her on the arm as if she were a mentally challenged child. "India, you're the one he's going to marry. Do you mean to tell me you're going to let a silly misunderstanding come between you marrying a fine, upstanding young man like Steven? He was just featured in *Ebony* magazine as one of the most eligible bachelors in the country. He'll eventually run for public office like his father. Not only is he politically connected, his family has money. A lot of it! Use the good sense God gave you, child."

India should have known her parents wouldn't offer much in the way of support, especially when her decision had gone against their plans.

"Your mother is right, India. I'm sure you overreacted. Steven is a powerful man. There are bound to be times when he
10

needs to let off some steam."

Did she hear him correctly? Was her father telling her it was okay for Steven to cheat on her because he was successful? "Is that what you call it?" India snorted in disgust.

Trevor rolled his eyes. "You can't expect people in Steven's world to be completely faithful. He is a man, after all. You should be grateful someone like him wanted you. Think about it, girl, you're not going to get better than him again."

What a thing to say to one's daughter. If she weren't so used to this from her parents, it would hurt far more than it did.

Her head began to throb. Arguing with her parents was like banging her head into a brick wall. "Look, I'm going home. You're obviously not going to support my decision, which by the way is final, so there's no point in continuing this conversation." India walked to the couch where she'd left her jacket and collected it along with her purse.

Her father tried to stall her. "We're not through talking to you, India."

She snatched her arm away. "But I'm through talking about it. Goodnight." She didn't stop walking until she made it to her car, despite their calls for her to come back.

There was no pleasing them. It wasn't enough that she'd gotten good grades, graduated at the top of her class, held a law degree and a respectable job, or that she'd done everything they'd ever asked of her. No matter how hard she tried to be what they wanted, she couldn't.

India's parents had let her know in none too subtle ways she'd been unwanted—an "oops" who'd come along in their lives when they should have been enjoying their golden years together.

Trevor and Leila Powers had been happy in their family of

three until she'd come along. They'd already had their one perfect child in Jack. He could do no wrong. She on the other hand could do no right. Growing up, it had hurt seeing how much more they cared for her unappreciative brother, beaming at every single nonachievement in his life, while she had to do headstands to get their attention.

They'd gone out of their way to attend all of Jack's events, but found excuses not to do the same for her. Even when she'd gone through her rebellious stage, they barely batted an eye.

In adulthood, it was India who ran errands for them and who was there when they needed a favor, but was it even acknowledged? Never. When Jack decided to grace them with his presence, which was rare, her parents were all smiles.

It was one thing to feel one's parents loved their sibling more than them, but it was quite another to know it was true.

Only when she'd begun dating Steven Cartwright did they seem to take an interest in her life. Besides Jack, there was nothing her parents loved more than one-upping their friends and family. They had to have the best house, buy the most expensive cars and go on the most exotic vacations, even if their incomes didn't always support their extravagance.

India's engagment to such a prominent up-and-comer had been a feather in their caps. Of course she'd been flattered to have someone like Steven take an interest in her. He was good looking, polished and smart—all great qualities. It was too bad he couldn't keep it in his pants. Catching him cheating brought all the uncertainties she'd dealt with throughout their relationship to the forefront. It made her wonder whether she would have gone through with the wedding had she been none the wiser. If India was being completely honest with herself, she wasn't sure if she'd agreed to marry him because she loved him or because her parents liked him so much.

Regardless, they were through. Her mother may be willing to accept infidelity to maintain her way of life, but India wasn't prepared to do the same.

When she made it to her apartment there were three messages on her answering machine. Against her better judgment, she checked them.

"India, I don't know what the hell got into you tonight, but you have a lot of explaining to do. You embarrassed me in front of my friends, colleagues and family. Once I calm my parents down, who have been nothing but nice to you by the way, I'm coming over to straighten this mess out." Steven practically yelled the message.

Was he kidding? His mother was a holy terror. Sure she was nice to her "baby", but when no one was around Mrs. Cartwright let her know in no uncertain terms India wasn't good enough for her precious Steven.

Mr. Cartwright was no better, constantly talking to her in a condescending manner, and putting down her job as a public defender. What bothered her most about him were the "accidents". The first time he touched her booty, his hand supposedly slipped, but the second and third time was beyond enough. Telling Steven about it had done nothing to change matters.

Good riddance to the lot of them. Anyway, Steven was sadly mistaken if he thought she'd allow him to cross her threshold.

The cheating bastard.

"India, sweetheart, this is your Aunt Val. I'm just checking in to see if everything is alright If you're up to it, give me a call and let me know if you're okay."

A slight smile touched her lips. Good ole' Aunt Val, always there when India needed her.

"India Rochelle Powers, you have a lot of nerve walking out

on your father and I after the stunt you pulled tonight—"

India pushed the button to shut off the message. She didn't need this. The only person she was inclined to call back was her aunt.

Picking up the receiver, she punched in Aunt Val's number.

"Hello?"

"Aunt Val, it's me, India."

"Hey, sweetheart. I'm glad you called. I was worried about you. How are doing?" There were no recriminations in her tone nor did she demand to know why India had done it.

And she appreciated it.

India sighed. "Pretty good, considering I was just tag-teamed by Mom and Dad. They weren't happy about what I did."

Her aunt chuckled. "Well, standing up in the middle of the toast to tell the guests you weren't going to marry...uh, a no good son of a bitch, according to you, at your engagement dinner was bound to create some drama. I'm sure you had a good reason though. It's not my place to judge."

The tears that had threatened to spill earlier flowed down her cheeks. To have someone in her corner meant so much to her after all she'd been through today. She sniffed. "Thank you, Aunt Val. And yes, I did have a good reason, although Mom and Dad don't think so. I remembered I left my jacket at Steven's place and when I went over, I spotted his car in the driveway, but he'd told me he'd be in court all day. I don't know why, but I got a funny feeling, so I let myself in with his spare key. I heard noises coming from his bedroom and to make a long story short, I saw Steven in bed with some woman."

Her aunt gasped. "That asshole! What did he say when you caught him?"

India's face burned with humiliation as she remembered what she'd seen. "Nothing. He didn't see me standing in the doorway. I left the house before he could. I probably should have told him before the dinner, but..."

"But what, baby?"

"I knew how upset my parents would be."

Val snorted. "My sister doesn't use the two brain cells she was given and your father—those two deserve each other. Leila has been putting on airs since we were kids. If we didn't look so much alike I would wonder if one of us was adopted."

India wondered the same thing herself. The rest of her family was so down to Earth. "They are my parents, so I guess I'm stuck with them."

"Unfortunately," Val said in a deadpan voice. "What are you going to do now?"

"I don't know. I haven't thought this far. I still can't believe I did that."

"Maybe you should take a vacation. You can take a couple weeks off work can't you?"

The state did owe her some time off. India had been saving her vacation days for her honeymoon, but seeing how there was no point of that anymore, why not? "Yes, I actually have four weeks to take. I don't know if I'll take them all at once, but going away might be a good idea."

"Most definitely. Besides, as I've said before, there comes a time when you realize that you can't please everyone all the time, so why not please yourself?"

That was the best thing India had heard all day.

ॐ

Eve Vaughn

"Are you going to be okay, Rafe? It's not every day a guy gets divorced." Grant patted his friend's shoulder.

Rafe shrugged. "Yeah, I'm okay. Angie and I have been over for months, but now it's official. I'm better off without her."

"You're probably right. I wish it hadn't cost you so much. She didn't deserve a dime after what she put you through."

Rafe sighed. "It's not as if I'm in the poorhouse. At least she took the lump sum instead of making me pay alimony for God knows how long. Besides, would you rather have had the intimate details of our marriage revealed for public record?"

Grant took another swig of his beer, finishing it off. "Is that why she was able to walk away with so much?"

A mutinous expression crossed Rafe's face.

Grant knew it well. After twenty-five years of friendship, he knew Rafe better than Rafe knew himself. "She threatened to name me in the divorce, didn't she?"

"Don't press the issue, man. I'd rather not talk about it at all. Don't concern yourself with it. Angie is out of my life—out of our lives."

Grant threw his hands in the air, frustration taking over. "How can I not concern myself with it? The two of you broke up because of me... I mean, I feel responsible."

Rafe shook his head. "No, you're not."

"But if we hadn't—"

Rafe held up his hand. "Grant, she was the one to break our agreement. What happened between the three of us should have stayed that way. What we did, didn't give her license to fuck every Tom, Dick and Harry—and on our bed, for godsake! What we shared was..."

"Special?" Grant finished for him.

16

There. It was out.

They'd both been avoiding the subject since Rafe had filed for divorce against his wife of three years. Regardless of what his friend said, Grant felt partially, if not completely, responsible for the split. He should have given the couple more space, not visited so much, not called as often. It had been clear from the beginning of Rafe's marriage that Angie resented the men's closeness.

The friendship he shared with Rafe was a bond tighter than most, even that of blood. It was hard for most people to understand, especially those on the outside looking in. Grant often wondered how different his life would have turned out if Rafe wasn't in it. He shuddered as the memories came flooding back.

They'd met not long after Rafe and his mother had moved next door to Grant and his father in Kensington, Philadelphia, a working class neighborhood. Grant had been startled awake by the sound of screaming coming from his neighbor.

"And stay out until you get some fucking manners!" The yell was followed by the slamming of the door.

In most circumstances Grant would have ignored the commotion, but for some reason, curiosity got the better of him. Looking back, he was glad it did, because if he'd pretended not to hear the other boy's cries drifting to his window, there probably wouldn't have been a friendship.

The opportunity would have been lost. They would have gone on with their lives, both of them barely scraping through everyday, praying for death or for someone to come take them from their own private hells.

Rafe had become his friend from that moment on. They were each other's support when Grant's father had too much to drink or when Julio got into a touchy-feely mood. Grant honestly believed he would have died if it had not been for his friend, because so many times he wanted to take his own life, especially when he felt his father's fists pounding into him. The experience could have turned him bitter and angry, but he had Rafe to get through those lean years.

Grant's prayers were eventually answered when he was fifteen. His father was arrested for felony assault, stemming from a bar fight. Grant was placed in a foster home. Ironically, Rafe became a ward of the state later that year as well, when his mother found a boyfriend who wanted marriage, but didn't want to be saddled with a teenage son. Almost as if fate had intervened, the two of them wound up in the same foster home.

They made a pact with each other to not allow what had happened in their pasts to consume them and make something of themselves. With the other's support and encouragement, they paid their way through college and found good jobs in their fields of accounting, all while pursing their MBAs. They eventually opened their own firm, which was now a huge success.

Grant considered Rafe his family and he knew his friend felt the same.

"It was more than special," Rafe finally answered, bringing Grant back to the present. He dragged his fingers through his thick brown hair. "The only thing missing was someone who truly cared about the both of us. Angie wasn't that person. The only one she loved was herself."

Grant lifted a brow. "Are you saying what I think you are? You've come up with some pretty wild ideas in our lifetime, but this?"

"Come on, Grant. You can't tell me you didn't enjoy it. When there were three of us, the sex was amazing, but it could be so much better with the right person. Think about it. What if we found someone who didn't mind—"

Grant held up his hands. "Whoa. Now you're talking crazy. What woman would go for that? With our damn luck, we'd end up with another Angie, and that would basically leave us in the same boat we're in. Besides, it's not normal."

"According to whom? I'll be damned if I let someone else try to put a wedge between the two of us again. Especially when we both have a taste of how good things could be. Anyway, you're the one who brought it up. "

"No, technically you did. I was simply finishing your statement."

"But you wouldn't have been able to do it if you weren't thinking along the same lines as me. Look man, I've given this some thought in the past several weeks, and I've come to the conclusion sharing a woman would be to our benefit."

"And say we do find someone else to go along with our plan, what's in it for her?"

"She'd get twice the love and attention."

Grant rubbed his chin, trying to take everything in. "Hmm, I don't know about this. How do we know she'd remain content with the arrangement? Or that she's not just looking for a cheap thrill."

Rafe's eyes narrowed. "Why do you keep coming up with excuses for not doing this? Call me crazy, but I think we'll know her when we see her."

The corner of Grant's lips curled. "As simple as that? It may work if we were in a movie, but this is real life."

"That's right. And impossible things don't happen right? Like two kids overcoming their crummy circumstances when statistics say we should either be dead, in jail or abusers ourselves."

Grant could hardly argue with that logic. He could tell from the mutinous look on his friend's face, Rafe was dead serious and once his mind was made up there was rarely any changing it. Besides, Grant realized he did indeed enjoy sharing a woman with his best friend—his brother. Did that make them perverts?

On some level, it had brought them closer together. As Rafe had pointed out, things could be so much better with the right woman. He was probably right, after all, Grant had enjoyed the threesome with Angie, a woman who at best he'd tolerated. He could only imagine how exciting things could be with a women he loved as much as Rafe.

"But what if we can't agree on a woman?"

A wide grin tilted Rafe's mouth.

Grant groaned. "You're up to something."

"Not at all. My divorce was just finalized. There's no rush in finding Ms. Right."

"So what do we do until then?"

"We'll have fun with a bunch of Ms. Right Nows in the meantime."

Chapter Two

India had the distinct impression someone was watching her. She squirmed in her chair, feeling self-conscious. She looked to her right and found herself staring into a pair of the most beautiful eyes she'd ever seen—cat eyes, a dark gold ringed with black, framed with thick, dark lashes.

Her breath caught in her throat. Had the temperature just gone up? She quickly looked away from him, and grabbed her travel itinerary. She didn't come on this trip to meet men. This was strictly for relaxing, lying out on the beach and drinking fruity beverages with little paper umbrellas in them.

Even if Mr. Sexy over there was by far one of the most good-looking men she'd seen.

Aunt Val had convinced India to take a vacation and now she was glad she had. Steven was relentless in his pursuit of her and she was tired of the nasty messages on her answering machine from her parents. India wished she had normal parents like everyone else. It would be nice to know she had the support of the two people who were supposed to love her unconditionally.

India often wondered if things would have been different if she'd been born a boy. But none of it mattered anymore. India intended to leave her problems behind. She looked at the brochure for the resort her travel agent had booked. It seemed like paradise. Fuamatuu Island was just off the coast of Australia, a relatively new vacation spot that not many people had yet discovered. All the better for her. The less people, the more she'd enjoy it. Having experienced a fifteen hour plane trip with one more flight to go, she couldn't wait to leave this cramped little airport.

She sighed, imagining herself snorkeling, parasailing, scuba-diving and horseback riding...some of the amenities the resort offered.

"Interesting reading material?" A deep voice broke into her thoughts.

She didn't have to look up to know who stood over her. The scent of his cologne drifted to her nostrils, titillating her senses. The little voice in her head told India to ignore him, but against her better judgment she tilted her head. A gasp escaped her lips before she could catch it.

When he'd only been a couple feet away from her she knew he was gorgeous, but up close, there wasn't an adequate word to describe this god standing before her. Again those golden eyes of his held her mesmerized. Thick dark brown brows slashed over his eyes gave him a somewhat sinister look, but somehow they suited him.

A long patrician nose rested above full, sensual, red lips slightly tilted in a lopsided grin. His hair fell in soft careless waves around his head. His light bronze skin gave away his Latin ancestry. The rugged cut of his face saved him from the label of pretty boy. Tall and broad, he was the epitome of drop-dead gorgeous.

If his sinewy arms were anything to go by, she was sure his body was as magnificent as the rest of him. Tall and Sexy took the empty seat next to her. "Do you mind?" His smile widened to reveal even white teeth.

Was there anything on this man that wasn't perfect? "Huh? Uh...no, I don't mind." What a total idiot she was. Twenty-eight years old and tongue-tied around a man.

"I'm usually not this forward, but since you were sitting by yourself..." He held out his hand to her. "Rafe Santiago."

"India Powers." She took the offered hand and shook it, but when she would have pulled hers away, he held on. "Um, you can let go of my hand now."

His eyes twinkled. "Must I?"

"Yes, you must." This time when she tugged her hand, he let go.

"Pity."

Normally she would have brushed off such a blatant come-on, but something about this guy wouldn't allow her. Sheesh. She and Steven were barely broken up and already she was ogling some stranger in an airport. If her ex-fiancé could hurt her, there was no telling the devastation this hottie would cause. It was probably best to nip this acquaintance in the bud. "When I said I didn't mind you sitting next to me, I didn't invite you to hit on me."

Instead of being chastised, he seemed amused. "I apologize, but when I saw you sitting here by yourself, I couldn't help but wonder what a beautiful woman is doing alone on a trip like this."

He was a smooth one, which meant she'd have to strengthen her resolve.

"Enjoying the solitude."

"Touché."

India resumed looking at her brochure, hoping he'd get the hint, but the weight of his stare burned her skin. With a sigh she put the brochure down. "You're not going away, are you?"

"Do you want me to?"

Lord, he was gorgeous. The smile he gave her was contagious, because she found herself grinning back.

"That's more like it. You have a lovely smile."

"I'm sure you say that to all the girls, Romeo."

"Only when it's true."

The heat rose to her cheeks. She'd been complemented on her looks before, but coming from Rafe it seemed different. Maybe a little harmless vacation flirtation wouldn't be a bad thing. "So, Rafe, I take it you're also alone on this trip. Why are you flying solo?"

"Actually, I'm not. I'm with my best friend. He's getting something to eat, but he should be back shortly. I think you'd like him."

"If he's a Casanova like you, I think I'm in trouble." She had to be nuts. Only minutes ago, she'd decided to brush him off, yet here she was acting like a schoolgirl with her first crush.

"Actually, Grant has a more laid-back approach when it comes to the ladies, but I think you'll like him. You're going to Fuamatuu as well?"

She waved her brochure in front of him. "How did you guess?"

He chuckled. It was a wonderful sound. "Okay, I caught a peek at it. Since we're going to the same destination, maybe we could meet up for drinks."

Should she? Part of her wanted to throw caution to the wind, while the practical half screamed "caution.". "That sounds nice, but..."

"But?"

The cautious side won. "I don't want this to come out the wrong way, but I want to keep things on a strictly friends-only basis. While it would be nice to have a couple people to hang out with while I'm there, I'm not ready for anything else."

Rafe gave her a long questioning look before speaking again. "Who was he?"

India furrowed her eyebrows together. "What do you mean?"

"The man who put that sad look in your eyes. Besides your beauty, it was one of the first things I noticed. What you just said confirmed my suspicions."

Most times, India had a difficult time opening up to people, but Rafe put her at ease for reasons she couldn't explain. "Up until a week ago I was engaged to be married. Things didn't work out."

"What happened?" He gave her a sheepish smile. "Sorry. I'm being intrusive."

"It's okay. He was unfaithful. I'm probably better off without him."

Rafe nodded. "He sounds like a real winner, not to mention an idiot for letting someone like you slip away. But I guess you and I are in the same boat. My divorce was recently finalized."

She touched his shoulder in sympathy. "Did she cheat on you?"

His brief pause gave India the answer. "It's a little more complicated, but yes, you can say she did." There was something cryptic in his statement, but India decided not to press.

"I brought you a sandwich, Rafe."

India looked in the direction of the newcomer, to see a blond man carrying a take-out bag. Though he didn't have Rafe's classic good looks, his craggy features had a quality about them that would make any woman look twice. His face was full of character, from his high cheekbones, pale blue eyes and the deep cleft in his chin. He reached at least six feet, not as tall as Rafe, but he was broader and more muscularly built.

Their eyes locked and his immediately cut away from hers.

"Thanks, Grant." Rafe took the take-out bag from his friend. "Grant, this is India. She's headed for Fuamatuu Island too, so we'll probably be seeing a lot of her there."

"Nice to meet you, India." Grant gave her a smile that lit up his entire face. It made him quite handsome.

"You as well." She briefly shook his offered hand before snatching hers away. "Umm, I think I'm going to the restroom to freshen up."

She gathered her carry-on and hopped up, not bothering to look back as she practically flew down the airport corridor.

What the hell was wrong with her? It was bad enough to be sexually aware of one man, but not two. Maybe these strange feelings she was experiencing were due to the lack of sex in the past several months. Steven had insisted they remain celibate until they were married.

He had convinced her it would make their wedding night more romantic. What a joke that turned out to be. While she'd been suffering through her dry spell, he'd been humping his mystery lady and probably anything in a skirt. Still, why had she reacted to those two men the way she had? Perhaps she was just being silly, but India couldn't remember a time when she'd been so drawn to any man, let alone two like she was with Rafe and Grant.

India made her way to the restroom and walked to the sink. She splashed water on her face. "Guess you needed this vacation more than you thought," she said to her reflection.

It was almost like looking at a stranger. The dark, shoulder length hair she once sported was now a chin-length bob, tucked

26

behind her ears. Her new hairstyle made her dark brown eyes look huge. Her mocha-colored skin had a grayish tint. It was probably from the stress she'd been under the past couple of weeks. She certainly didn't feel like the beautiful woman Rafe claimed she was.

A late bloomer, India had once been skinny and awkward with a bad complexion, something else her parents had disparaged over. It was only in her late teens that her body gained the womanly curves she now sported, and her skin cleared up. Braces corrected her teeth and she'd grown more comfortable in her body, however her improved looks had once again become an issue.

Instead of being the butt of cruel jokes, men were acting like idiots around her. India had never quite shaken off the stigma of being an ugly duckling. It was probably why Steven wanted her. She had the right look—the perfect arm piece for his ambitions. And he'd probably recognized her insecurities and used them to manipulate her.

Now that the blinders were off, India was determined to live her life according to her own rules. No longer would she give in to the demands of her parents or allow a man to swallow her identity. It was finally her turn to live, starting with this vacation. Why run away from Rafe and Grant?

"What did you think of her?" Rafe asked between bites of his sandwich.

Grant didn't answer right away. A thoughtful expression crossed his face. "Gorgeous, but..."

"Not your type?" Rafe held his breath in anticipation of his friend's answer. He knew Grant gravitated toward willowy

27

redheads, but the way he had stared at India told Rafe there may be some interest there.

"It's not that. I'd imagine she's every man's type. I was watching you two talk for a few good minutes before I approached. I couldn't stop staring at her—those lips and eyes...she's a stunner."

"So what's the problem?"

Grant shrugged. "Come on, Rafe, need you ask? Women fall over their feet to get near you. Me on the other hand—they seem to lose interest when you enter the picture. I definitely think India is way out of my league. Besides, she may not be into white guys. You saw how she bolted when I joined the two of you."

Rafe shook his head. "I didn't get the impression she cared about something so trivial. Anyway, aren't we all black when the lights are out?"

That comment brought a slow smile to Grant's face. "I suppose we are, but it doesn't mean she'd be interested in me. The last woman I really cared about...well, we both know how that ended."

Yeah. Rafe ended up marrying her. Guilt pierced his conscience. Since he and Grant had hit puberty and discovered girls, there was a friendly competition between the two of them where the fairer sex was concerned.

No matter whom the victor had been, neither let a female come between them. Most of their twenties had been spent in school and building their accounting firm. There hadn't been much time for women until they'd become successes, but when they did, their skirt chasing grew more intense.

Angie had done a number on the both of them, almost destroying their friendship in the process, until her machinations finally backfired. Rafe should have known Angie was trouble when she'd come for financial advice. She had, after all, been looking to invest a small inheritance from her deceased husband, who Rafe later learned had been eighty-eight years old. He'd found that little tidbit out too late.

Had he known that, he never would have gotten involved with her outside of their business meetings, but the little head had taken over the big one. A platinum blonde with a body that didn't quit, she wasn't the most beautiful woman he'd ever seen, but Angie definitely knew how to work what she had—and boy did she! They began dating almost immediately. So caught up in the whirlwind of their romance, Rafe didn't realize the subtle things she did to keep him from spending time with Grant.

She'd made it plain from the beginning of their relationship that she wouldn't tolerate him giving anyone other than her his attention. Looking back, Rafe should have known how things would be, but instead he'd become more deeply involved with her

It wasn't long before she brought the subject of marriage up, but Rafe had not been ready. Out of spite, she went after Grant, who Rafe then discovered had secretly had a crush on her all along. For the first time since they'd become friends, there was tension between them. She pitted them against each other until finally Rafe believed he couldn't live without her. He broke down and asked her to marry him—what she'd been angling for all along.

Once the ring was on her finger, Angie systematically set out to destroy Rafe and Grant's bond. Grant stayed away because Angie would flirt shamelessly, teasing and taunting him, sometimes making unnecessary sexual innuendoes. Rafe shuddered when he remembered all the fights he and his ex had when he wanted to hang out with his friend outside of work. It eventually became an even bigger strain between him and Grant.

After a while, the sex with Angie wasn't worth coming home for. He found himself staying late at the office just to have some peace. It wasn't as if he hadn't tried to keep her happy, but whatever he did wasn't enough, at least not for his wife. Scenes from the night that had changed their lives ran through his mind.

Rafe and Grant and gone out for some drinks after work with a few of their employees. They'd stayed out later than he intended. Grant had offered him a ride home because Rafe had had too many drinks to be comfortable behind the wheel of a car. When he pulled up to the house, he remembered he had some paperwork he wanted to give to Grant and asked him to come inside. The moment they walked in the door, they were confronted by an apparently furious Angie.

"Well, well, well, you finally made it back and this time you have the audacity to bring that man into my house." Her words were slurred, making it obvious he wasn't the only one who'd been drinking that night.

"This is my house too, and Grant is welcome in it anytime he wants to come over."

She glared at him. "So that's how it is? I should have known."

"What the hell are you talking about, Angie?" Rafe demanded.

"Did your friend tell you he tried to come on to me?"

Rafe looked at Grant, whose face had turned beet red.

"That's not true. I haven't touched you since you became engaged to Rafe. For once tell the damn truth. It was the other way around. You've been making advances toward me."

Rafe rarely saw Grant lose his temper and he was more

inclined to believe his friend. "Angie, I don't have time for your dramatics tonight." He tried to walk past her, but she grabbed his arm.

"You believe him over me? Your own wife? Maybe this *friendship*," she used air quotes, "you have is a little more than you claim it to be." Angie had said some vicious things before, but this was outside of enough.

Rafe narrowed his eyes. "Are you implying what I think you are?"

Angie laughed with a maniacal gleam in her eyes. "Why not? You barely touch me anymore and you're always with him." She pointed to Grant. "The courts would be sympathetic toward me when they find out I've been married to a pillow biter who married me to cover up his homosexual affair."

"Shut your mouth, you bitch!" Rafe raged.

She sneered. "Make me."

Rafe didn't know what made him do it, especially with Grant standing there, but he slammed Angie against the wall and covered her mouth in an angry kiss. He tore at her clothing, his anger driving him.

She returned his ardor with vehemence, gripping his shirt to bring him closer. Angie eventually tore her mouth away from his and looked over his shoulder to stare at Grant, who was walking out the door. "Where the hell are you going? Get your ass over here," she commanded.

Rafe stiffened. Everything that had been instilled within him about the fundamentals of monogamy screamed how wrong her suggestion was. But there was another part of him that wanted to know what it would be like to share a woman with his best friend. Maybe it was the alcohol or perhaps it was some deep-seated fantasy he'd had all along, but he found himself looking at Grant. "Give her what she wants."

Grant's mouth gaped open. "I...I can't."

Angie's smile was malicious. "Hmm, I suppose I was right about one of you then. You were always such a...*gentleman* when we dated." She made the word gentleman seem like a dirty word.

It was just the thing to get Grant riled. He strode over to them and grabbed Angie. The next thing Rafe knew, the three of them were in bed. Grant and Rafe sucked, licked and fucked Angie throughout the hours of the night. It had been one of the most sexually fulfilling moments he'd ever experienced. Then it started. For months they shared his wife until Rafe discovered he and Grant weren't the only ones she was screwing.

Rafe had come home one day to find her in bed with four men.

Angie didn't look embarrassed at being caught. "You only have yourself to blame. This is what you started," she'd said in her defense.

It was in that moment he realized he didn't love her and never had. What had made the experience of his threesome so meaningful was his best friend...not her. It was easy to walk away from the marriage once he'd figured that out.

Rafe's subsequent divorce to Angie had affected them both.

"Grant, I know she said some nasty things to you toward the end, but you've been through too much—we've been through too much to let her destroy us now. She's out of our lives and it's time to turn the page to a new chapter. I have a feeling this will be a memorable vacation and India Powers will figure heavily into it."

Grant didn't look so sure. "If you say so."

"I do, my friend."

Chapter Three

India hadn't been on many planes in her life, but she knew enough to know something wasn't right. Granted this was a commuter jet, smaller than she was used to, with a maximum seating capacity of sixteen. Currently it only carried nine, including the pilot and flight attendant.

The clanging engine sputtered, then it made a whizzing noise. What the hell was going on?

She looked to the flight attendant for assurance, but was met with a look of worry. Okay, now was the time to get flustered. Sitting across from her on the other side of the aisle were the two men she'd met in the airport. "What's going on?" She mouthed the words to them.

Grant shrugged. Rafe, on the other hand, kept looking out the window with a frown on his face.

It didn't help matters that it had begun raining and she could feel every air pocket the plane hit. If only the captain would speak up and tell them everything would be okay, her heart wouldn't beat so fast. It was as if someone had read her mind because the announcement finally came.

"Ladies and gentlemen of flight 2692, we're experiencing some engine trouble. I ask that everyone remain calm. As you can see, the fasten seatbelt sign is on so please remain seated with your seatbelts securely fastened. Remember, in case of a water landing, your seat can be used as a floatation device."

That did nothing to calm her already intense nerves.

"We're all going to die," a frantic passenger screamed from the seat directly in front if India's. It was bad enough being on such a little plane, but when people started panicking, it only made the situation worse.

"Shut up, you ninny!" a man yelled at the hysterical woman.

India griped her arm rests. "Please don't freak out. Please don't freak out," she chanted to herself.

Suddenly the coughing and sputtering of the engine stopped, followed by the feeling of falling.

Now she could freak out. India closed her eyes and said a silent prayer. From this height, no one would survive the impact. Just then the engine started to jerk violently, but it was too late—chaos had already broken out on the tiny plane. A few of the passengers were crying and screaming. She clutched the armrests, her heart beating erratically and nerves on edge. If this was how she was going to die, India didn't want it to be without the touch of another human.

Perhaps it was the desperation of the situation, or it could have been that she had made a brief connection when she'd looked over to Grant and Rafe, but for whatever reason, India reached across the aisle and took Grant's hand, his large palm engulfing hers.

Their eyes locked and then Rafe grabbed both of their hands, and squeezed.

A sense of peace settled over her. She never imagined her last moments would be spent on a plummeting plane while holding hands with two strangers. But she was okay with it.

"Ladies and gentlemen, the backup engine has kicked in and I'm going to attempt a water landing." The captain didn't sound so sure about his decision. A water landing...in the middle of the friggin' Pacific? What if the water was infested with sharks, and how far away were they from land?

Who was to say the plane wouldn't sink and they'd all drown? She closed her eyes tight, wishing she hadn't spent her life trying to please her parents. When India thought about the choices she'd made in her life, they all revolved around them. She probably wouldn't have gotten engaged to Steven. India had thought she loved him, but now she realized she had loved the idea of being with him because he represented the one thing that would make her family happy.

The plane jolted and jumped, but the plummeting had slowed down. India had a feeling the impact would still be big.

"Let me off!" screamed the man in the front seat of the plane.

To India's horror, he unfastened his seat belt and jumped out of his seat.

"You can't do that," the crying lady behind her yelled.

The poor flight attendant, white as a sheet, looked like she'd pass out with terror.

With each bobble and jostle of the plane, India's seatbelt tightened around her waist, cutting her air supply. Where were the oxygen masks? Shouldn't they have fallen already? It seemed the engine wasn't the only thing malfunctioning on this godforsaken hunk of junk.

The crazed man who had been sitting in the front got out of his seat and grabbed the latch.

Holy shit. He was going to open the door. If any of them had the slimmest chance of survival, he was doing his damnedest to eliminate that as well.

"No!" she cried out. India couldn't sit there passively and watch this lunatic kill them any faster. She had to do something. With her free hand she unclipped her seatbelt.

Grant squeezed her hand. "What the hell are you doing? Put that back on."

"Look at him! He's going to get us all killed." She tried to tug her hand out of their collective grips.

Rafe looked as if he would add his two cents, but the words never came, because the door flew open, creating a vacuum within the cabin. The man who opened the door was instantly pulled out of the plane. India was sucked forward, causing her to slam into the seat in front of her. Hard.

She tried to put her belt back on, but it was too late. The pressure in the cabin was too great to move, and her world started to spin from lack of oxygen and the hit to her head. It was a nightmare come true.

The sound of splintering metal made a sickening crunch. The plane was ripping apart, but by now India had grown too woozy to care. Her eyelids were heavy and she couldn't keep them open.

Panic ensued all around her and someone was holding on to her arm, while she experienced the feeling of being sucked out of her seat. Her last conscious thought before passing out was, at least she'd go out with a bang.

ॐ

"I think she's still breathing." The relief in Rafe's voice mirrored Grant's feelings. Just before the crash, he'd gripped her so tight she couldn't go anywhere. She had passed out, but Grant held on.

He wished all the passengers and crew had made it, but not all had been so fortunate. The flight attendant was among the casualties from what Grant had determined. The plane hit the turbulent ocean, but as luck would have it, the pilot maneuvered the vehicle low enough to the water's surface so the impact wasn't fatal.

The next major hurdle they'd faced was getting out of the place without drowning because once the plane was fully submerged, there would be no escaping. Ironically, it was the open hatch that saved them. The brave pilot had taken charge, enlisting Grant and Rafe's assistance because there was no other crew to help him through this horrific dilemma.

They helped dismantle the seats and hustle everyone out. Then Grant grabbed the unconscious India with Rafe's aide, and jumped into the water, not knowing what would happen next. It had been an effort staying afloat with the angry waves crashing into his body while he held on to India. The next hurdle they all had to overcome was figuring out how the hell they'd get out of the middle of the ocean.

In his attempt to save one of the passengers, the pilot was taken under with the flailing woman. Every time he'd come up, she'd pull him back under. Rafe tried to help, but he too became caught in the melee and went under as well.

"No!" Grant had screamed, torn between holding on to India and going to Rafe. Luckily he didn't have to make that decision because Rafe resurfaced. The pilot and the woman, however, did not.

There were only five of them left and hope was fading fast. The water was cold and the rain beat against them. Grant knew he wouldn't be able to hold on to India and stay above surface indefinitely. Their only hope was to find land.

The hand of fate appeared when hope was quickly

dwindling. The rain stopped and the clouds opened up to reveal the sun. At first Grant thought he'd imagined it, but off in the distance he saw a sliver of land.

Hope.

Once he pointed to what he'd seen, Grant somehow found the strength to propel himself and India toward the tiny island, but by the time they made it to land, they'd lost another passenger. Only four were left and from the looks of the prone man lying a few feet away, Grant didn't know if that number would remain.

"India, can you hear me?" Grant shook her shoulders in an attempt to rouse her. Was it wrong for him to notice how beautiful she was even in this state? Her hair was plastered to her forehead and cheeks, all makeup had been washed away from her face, and she was soaked. Still, he couldn't remember seeing anyone lovelier. He wondered how she'd react if he bent over and pressed his lips against hers. What the hell was wrong with him? This wasn't an appropriate line of thinking. He immediately pushed those thoughts away.

She groaned, her head moving from side to side.

"Yes. Thank goodness, she's alive."

He felt her body for any broken bones. There was a golf-ball-size lump on her forehead, but other than that he saw no visible signs of damage.

She released another groan before her eyes fluttered open. "Am I dead?" India's voice was a hoarse whisper.

"If you are, then so are we," Rafe answered, moving to her other side.

India tried to sit up, and winced. "My head feels like someone took a sledgehammer and hit me with it." She attempted to sit up again, but Grant stopped her.

"No. Don't make any sudden moves. You have a pretty nasty looking lump on your head. Do you feel any pain anywhere other than your head?"

She grimaced. "My side aches a little, but it doesn't bother me as much as my head."

Grant frowned with concern. He didn't like the looks of that lump, but at least she was coherent. He slowly helped her sit up. "Is that better?"

India tucked her hair behind her ears, and touched her head. "A little." She looked around her. "Where are we? Where are the rest of the passengers?"

Rafe took her hand in his. "There...there's only four of us left. As for where we are, I'm not sure. From the brief exploration I've done, there doesn't seem to be any inhabitants. I didn't go very far, so I could be wrong."

India's mouth formed an "O" as if she were trying to process what she'd just been told. "Only four survivors?" Her eyes glistened with the suspicious gleam of unshed tears.

Rafe pulled her against him. "It's okay. We'll be rescued in no time."

She pushed Rafe away and struggled to her feet. "No. It's not okay. How do we know someone will rescue us? Have you ever seen *Gilligan's Island? Lost? Cast Away?*" She looked as if she'd go into a full bout of hysterics.

Grant and Rafe stood up at the same time. When Grant reached out to touch her, she flinched away. "No, please don't."

Grant sighed. "India, that's television. This is reality. Someone will come for us."

She shook her head. "Don't patronize me. Look, I just need a minute to process this." India wrapped her arms around her body and walked a few feet away from them, her head hung low.

"Should we go to her?" Rafe asked.

Grant shook his head. "No. Give her a little time. We've had longer to get used to the situation than she's had."

Rafe snorted his derision. "Not by much. My watch is dead but we couldn't have been here longer than a half hour. I don't want to be a pessimist, but how do we know someone will come for us?"

Grant raked his fingers through his still damp hair. "I don't know much about planes, but don't they send out some kind of signal when they go down? Besides, when the plane doesn't arrive at its destination, I'm sure they'll send out a search party of some sort."

Rafe still didn't look completely convinced, but finally, he nodded. "That makes sense. How's Ralph doing?"

Grant had nearly forgotten him. The only other survivor who had made it to the island had collapsed. He was still breathing, but they couldn't rouse him. He had dubbed him Ralph because of his uncanny appearance to Ralph Kramden of *The Honeymooners*.

"I haven't checked on him in a few minutes."

Rafe walked over to the man. "Dammit!"

"What?" Grant wanted to know.

"He's dead."

Grant closed his eyes. There were now three of them, which meant they'd have to fight that much harder to survive. By some miracle Rafe, Grant and India had made it with minimal injuries.

"What should we do with the body?" Rafe asked.

"I don't know. We could push it out to the ocean."

Rafe wrinkled his nose. "That seems a little undignified."

India chose that moment to rejoin them. "We have to bury

him."

Rafe voiced his agreement, "Yes, that would probably be best, but from the looks of the sky, the sun will be setting shortly and things are going to get chilly pretty soon. I think we should hold off burying him until we find some wood to start a fire. Then we need to figure out how to get something to eat."

India shook her head with vehemence. There was a stubborn tilt to her chin. "No. We have to bury him now."

Grant thought Rafe's suggestion was a sensible one. "We can bury him as soon as we gather some supplies."

"No! We have to do it now!"

Rafe touched her shoulder. "Be reasonable. He's not going anywhere, but when it gets dark, there's not going to be much we can do."

India pulled away from him. "Fine. Then you two get supplies. I'll bury him." She wiped a tear away from her cheek and turned her back to them. Her movements were slow and jerky, making it obvious she still suffered some degree of pain. She bent over and grabbed Ralph's collar and attempted to pull him away, but she swayed from side to side as if she'd pass out.

Grant didn't understand her logic, but he had to admire her tenacity. He looked at his friend with a sigh. "We have to help her, Rafe. She's going to hurt herself, and frankly, I think she's not coping with this situation well."

"Neither am I, my friend, but you're right. If the three of us work at it, maybe we can still salvage some of the daylight."

They walked over to India, who was still struggling with the body. Grant gently nudged her aside. "We'll help. Just tell us the spot where you want him."

She pointed to a tree behind them. "Under there."

Grant lifted Ralph's body under the arms and Rafe took his

feet and they carried him to the spot indicated.

India knelt beside the body and started digging a hole with her hands, focused on her task. Grant knew they wouldn't be able to dig the hole wide or deep enough to put Ralph in before nightfall, but as he began to help her dig, he finally understood. Giving Ralph a proper burial somehow connected them to civilization.

They may be on a possibly deserted island, but participating in this act gave them a connection to the outside world. Grant didn't know how long they were at it, but it was well into the night before the three of them finished with the hole, placed Ralph in it, and covered the body.

None of them spoke for several moments until India finally broke the silence. "Does anyone want to say a few words about him?"

"I didn't know him, or his real name for that matter, but he seemed like a friendly guy when I talked to him briefly at the airport," Grant offered.

"Do you know the Lord's Prayer?" India asked.

Grant's upbringing gave him no reason to believe in a god, but before she'd died his mother had taught him when he was a boy. He wasn't religious, but did consider himself spiritual. "I know it, but I haven't said it in a while."

"And you, Rafe?" India questioned.

"Bits and pieces."

She nodded, seeming satisfied before taking Grant's and Rafe's hands in hers. "We'll say it together."

In unison they recited, "Our Father..."

By the end of the prayer, Grant was actually glad India had prodded them to do this. It felt right.

India stood up then with a shiver. "It's gotten cold, and it doesn't help that my clothes are still a little damp."

"It's probably too late to start looking for supplies, so we should look for someplace to sleep tonight. When I did a little exploring, I spotted a cave not too far from here. Looks like we'll have to huddle together to stay warm," Rafe suggested.

"That's probably a good idea," Grant agreed.

India didn't say anything, but she followed Rafe's lead to the shelter.

The cave was dark, dank and had an odd smell. Grant frowned wondering if it could get any worse. Almost as if he'd had some strange premonition, it started to rain again. It was followed by the crashing sound of thunder. The three of them went deeper into the cave.

"I hope we're the only ones in this cave. I'm not fond of the idea of being bear food."

Grant could only make out India's silhouette in the dark, but she sounded frightened.

"This isn't the right climate for bears. Wild boars maybe, but no bears," Rafe said.

"Gee, that's reassuring," India snorted.

"I think if we weren't alone, our hosts would have made their presence known by now," Grant assured her. "Come on, let's get some sleep. We're going to need all the rest we can get. How's the head, by the way?"

"Not as bad as before, but it still aches a little. I think by morning I should be fine."

They found a spot on the ground that wasn't too rocky. As suggested, they huddled together for warmth, with India in the middle.

Grant was bone tired, but the ground was hard and uncomfortable, not to mention India's curvaceous rear rested against his crotch. He willed his cock to stay down. He could have turned away, but didn't want to draw any attention to himself.

Here they were, survivors of a plane crash, not knowing when or if they'd be rescued, and he was trying to fight off his horniness. Grant was uncertain about their future on the island, especially when he didn't know how he'd get through the rest of the night.

Chapter Four

India stretched her arms over her head and lengthened her legs as far as they'd go in an attempt to alleviate the tension in her tight muscles. Her bed felt harder than usual, and there was a dull throb in the back of her head. Suddenly, she realized two solid bodies were pressed against hers, one of them lightly snoring.

Her eyes popped open. No! This had to be the continuation of her nightmare. She was still asleep. Yes, that was it. Closing her eyes again, India willed herself far away from the catastrophe she found herself embroiled in, but to no avail. The men resting against her were still there and in the distance, the sound of lapping waves hitting the sand greeted her ears.

"I won't cry. I won't cry," she chanted under her breath, allowing her lids to rise once again. Slowly, India eased into a sitting position, careful not to disturb the men. She ignored the tender ache in her arms and legs from sleeping on the hard ground all night. The events of the previous day hit her all at once.

She and her companions were on what appeared to be a deserted island, just like she was in some hokey movie or television program. Unlike Hollywood, however, there'd be no Professor making coconut radios, no blue lagoon, no volleyball companion, and no "Others" waiting to do God knows what with them. And most especially, there was no hope.

What did she know about surviving on an island? Hell, she'd never so much as been camping. What were they going to do and would they be rescued? India couldn't quite wrap her head around what had happened. It seemed so surreal.

Sliding from between Rafe and Grant, she managed to stand. The light seeping into the cave beckoned her to step outside. Once she hit the beach, India took a moment to look around her. If she had seen this place in a travel brochure she would have called it paradise. Its clear aqua waters beating against bleached white sand, the exotic looking vegetation further behind her, and tall trees with their large green leaves swaying in the gentle breeze would have been anyone's ideal getaway spot. Too bad this tropical island was now her virtual prison.

Would they die here? Remembering the body they'd buried the night before and imagining the same fate for herself sent a shiver up her spine. Just when she was ready to take charge of her life, fate stepped in and bitch-slapped her.

Wrapping her arms around her body, India fought back the tears.

"A penny for them," a voice broke into her thoughts.

She jumped. For a brief moment, she'd had such a sense of isolation; India had forgotten her fellow survivors. Turning, she saw Grant. Though not as striking as Rafe, Grant's blond, blue-eyed, All-American looks and tall, lean body were still quite pleasing to the eye. Her gaze slowly took in every detail of his face, committing it to memory, from the way a strand of his wavy locks fell over his forehead to his square jaw, down to the cleft in his chin. She'd always had a thing for guys with those.

Maybe he was a bit too pleasing to look at for her peace of

mind. Was it only yesterday she'd decided to flirt with both men? How ironic was it for the three of them to end up here together?

India took a step back from him, putting as much space between them as possible without making it too obvious. "We're on a deserted island, after surviving a plane crash. What do you think is on my mind?" she snapped before realizing how it must have sounded. It wasn't his fault they were in this situation. She sighed. "I'm sorry, it's just..."

"You're uncertain about how the three of us will get on."

She blinked. "Excuse me?" India blinked, wondering if she'd heard him correctly.

"How we're going to survive."

"Oh." Her cheeks grew hot. For a moment she thought he'd said how the three of them would get *it* on. Where in the world had that thought come from? She felt like an idiot and was thankful she hadn't said more.

Granted it had been a long time since she'd had sex, but now wasn't the appropriate time to allow her hormones to run rampant. Looking away from him, she tried to steer the conversation to safer territory. "Is Rafe awake?"

"He was just stirring when I got up. He's always been able to sleep like the dead, no matter where we are."

"You seem pretty familiar with his sleeping habits. Are you two—" India broke off, wanting to kick herself. Why did she keep putting her foot in her mouth? "I'm sorry. That's none of my business."

Grant threw his head back and released a loud belly laugh. "It's okay. No, we're not gay, just best friends; actually closer, like brothers, I'd say. We've known each other since we were kids and we were roommates in college. I can't tell you how many times I've crashed at his place and he mine for various

47

reasons, so I guess I would be familiar with his sleeping habits."

A faint smile touched her lips. She could very easily envy the special bond they shared. "It must be nice to have a close friend like that."

He raised a dark blond brow. "That was a wistful statement if I've ever heard one. Don't you have close friends?"

"Honestly? No. I was a bit of a loner in school. I was gangly, buck-toothed, awkward and shy. People weren't exactly lining up to be my friend."

"I find that hard to believe. A gorgeous woman like yourself?"

Most times she was uncomfortable with comments about her looks because in her mind, she was still the skinny, shapeless girl with no looks to speak of that she used to be, but from Grant, the words warmed her. She smiled. "You're sweet for saying so, but it's true. I didn't have many friends growing up. I was too busy trying to live up to the impossible standards my parents had set for me. Don't get me wrong, I've had friends, but a lot of them I've lost touch with over the years. I've made some good acquaintances I may occasionally see outside of work, but I haven't formed the kind of friendship you and Rafe obviously have."

"Did someone mention my name?"

As if she'd conjured him up, Rafe joined them on the beach. The stubble on his golden face was more pronounced this morning, and it only served to heighten his masculinity. Her heart beat faster. It was bad enough dealing with her attraction to Grant, but having the two of them next to her was doing things to her libido that she wouldn't have thought possible.

India crossed her arms over her chest, hoping they didn't notice her nipples tightening. "W-we were just talking about friends." She was unable to tear her gaze away from his macho, hair-roughened face.

Rafe gave her a brilliant white smile. "I hope you count me among one of yours."

"We barely know each other," she squeaked.

"Sweetheart, I have the feeling we'll be getting to know each other quite well, until we're rescued or find a way off this island."

India probably would have analyzed his prediction more closely had she not been reminded of their predicament. His words had her crashing back to reality. There was no telling whether they would find a way off or be found. She didn't want to panic, but her knees grew weak from nerves and her hands began to shake.

"Oh God, we're screwed." She bit her bottom lip to hold back a cry.

Grant strode over to India and gave her a gentle shake. "There's no point in taking that defeatist attitude. Yes, things look pretty grim right now, but I'm sure when the plane didn't arrive at its destination, someone would've sent some kind of search unit to scour the nearby islands for survivors. Until then, we'll need to gather supplies to hold us over." He pulled away, his hands falling from her arms as if he'd been shocked.

She'd felt it too. Unable to meet his gaze, she merely nodded in agreement.

"That makes sense," Rafe concurred. "I only hope it doesn't take too long for someone to find us.

India couldn't agree more. How would they last this far from civilization? What would they do for food? How would they bathe? A million questions ran through her mind, but she kept her thoughts to herself, not wanting to sound like a whiner. She was sure the two men had concerns of their own. Besides, complaining wouldn't help the situation.

She wrung her hands in front of her. "What do you suggest we do first? Maybe we could make a giant SOS sign in the sand?"

Grant nodded. "We can do that, but I think we should start looking for a fresh water supply. I know this isn't what anyone wants to hear, but we're going to need to prepare ourselves for a long stay."

India's heart sank. He was right. She didn't want to hear it.

Rafe's expression went bleak, but he simply rubbed his chin as though in deep thought; finally he said, "I believe I saw some coconut trees when we arrived here yesterday, so if that's the case, they'd supply us with both food and drink until we find something else."

Not wanting to be the only one to not contribute to the conversation she suggested, "We'll need fire. It was freezing last night."

"Good idea." Grant gave her a slow smile, revealing deep dimples. Lord, did he have to have a cleft and dimples? Were these men trying to send her into hormone overload? Now wasn't the time to notice how handsome either one of the men were because the situation didn't call for it. Different in looks as night and day, one with smooth Latin looks, while the other had the hot boy-next-door appeal, India realized her ass was in trouble.

She didn't realize she'd zoned out until Rafe snapped his fingers in her face. "Earth to India."

"Huh?"

Concern entered his amber eyes. "Are you okay? You looked a little lost there for a moment."

There was no way she was going to confess her true thoughts to them. "I uh...I was thinking we should probably get started before it gets too hot."

Grant's smile broadened. "That's a sensible idea. Beautiful and sharp as a tack."

"Well...I-I am a lawyer." Why did they have to flirt with her? Or was it her own overactive imagination playing with her mind, wanting there to be something there that wasn't?

"We won't hold that against you." Grant winked. "I was thinking we should begin as well. We'll probably need to split up so we can get things done faster. I read somewhere if you walk far enough along the shore line, you might find a stream or something like it that will lead to fresh water. I'll see how that pans out."

"I'll scavenge the island for food," Rafe volunteered.

"What should I do?" India hoped the men didn't intend on leaving her here to twiddle her thumbs.

"Collecting firewood would be helpful. I'm sure there are dead dry branches lying around the beach," Grant said.

India was thankful to be given a task to keep her occupied. The faster she was away from these two hunks, the sooner she'd be able to dispel her inconvenient carnal thoughts.

Rafe shook the tree, hoping to get another coconut to fall. He'd already collected three, but he wasn't sure it was enough. As hungry as he was, he could probably eat all three of them by himself. Not certain if the berries and plants he'd spotted were edible, he decided the sure bet would be to get as many of the coconuts as possible. Rafe hoped it was enough to hold them over for a few days. If they were here on this glorified sandbox longer than that, he'd have to see about catching fish. He shook the tree again with all his might, but the blasted things hung from the branches, mocking him.

He wondered if he could climb up the trunk and reach them. Rafe was contemplating how to make it up there when India sauntered over. Even with her hair in disarray and without makeup, she was stunning. One of her dress straps fell off one delectably curved shoulder. Rafe had always found something sexy about a woman's bare shoulders.

His body tightened as he took in her devastating curves. How he managed to keep his hands to himself with her body next to his was a miracle. The bodice of India's dress hung a little lower than it had the day before, revealing smooth chocolate mounds. His cock twitched at the sight she made.

How on Earth would he last on this island without touching her, pressing kisses all over her body, holding those lovely breasts in his hands and sliding his dick in and out of her tight pussy? Or maybe he'd sample some of that ass. She certainly had a nice one.

"I collected some firewood and put the pile a few feet away, but I have no idea how to start a fire."

Rafe wanted to start a fire within her. Shit, he silently cursed himself. Now wasn't the time to think with his dick. He finally found his voice after shaking away his horny thoughts. "Grant will know what to do."

"He seems very knowledgeable about what to do in a situation like this. Was he a Boy Scout?"

Rafe grinned. "Hardly. But he does enjoy the outdoors and he's gone on numerous camping trips."

"This is hardly the same."

"No, but he's probably a better go-to guy in this situation."

"You're not into the outdoors?"

Rafe chuckled with a shake of his head. "I enjoy my

creature comforts a little too much. Camping is Grant's way of unwinding. When we were kids, we used to sleep out in each other's backyards all the time. Sometimes we'd even hang out in the park all night when..." Even after all these years, his childhood still tore at his soul.

"When what?" she prompted gently.

"When we just wanted to get away," he muttered. He'd almost let slip how he and Grant would stay away from home a couple days at a time when Grant's father was having a drunken binge or when Rafe's mother brought home a new boyfriend. Rafe hadn't been as keen on staying outdoors as Grant had, but at least it was better than the alternative. India didn't need to hear it. She probably wouldn't be interested. How many times had Angie told him to get over it?

Maybe his ex-wife was right. His dysfunctional childhood was not something to be brought up in normal conversation even though these were far from normal circumstances.

"You were going to say something else."

She was too observant by far. "No. That was it."

India gave him a long shrewd look, telling him she didn't believe him, but she shrugged. "I notice you're having a problem getting that coconut down. Aren't those three enough?" She pointed to the ones on the ground.

"It wouldn't hurt to have a few more just in case. I was thinking of climbing up the tree to get those few that are dangling from that nearby branch. It looks like they're going to drop but the stubborn things won't fall."

"You can't climb up there and back down without getting scraped up. This bark is too rough. Why don't you give me a boost and I'll try to reach it?"

He studied the tree and judged the distance. "That just might work. If you can balance on my shoulders, I think you

53

might be able to reach that branch."

"There's only one way to find out." India smiled at him and Rafe melted. God, she was gorgeous.

Trying to keep his composure without making a total jackass of himself, he moved to the base of the tree and knelt, holding his clasped hands in front of him. "Okay, step up, my lady."

She moved toward him with a giggle. "I hope I'm not too heavy for you."

"I'm sure that won't be a problem. I'm much stronger than I look," he teased.

"That isn't what I was talking about and you know it."

"Don't worry, India, you'll be fine."

"If you're sure..."

"I am."

She stepped into his hands using the tree as leverage before he lifted her high enough to step on his shoulders.

Rafe gritted his teeth at the pressure, but it wasn't unbearable. He grasped India's ankles to keep her steady. She wobbled a bit, but he held her steady. Once she'd gained her balance, he waited a few minutes before asking, "Do you have it?"

"Almost. If you could move over just a tad to the left, I'll have it."

"Okay, hold on to the tree." Rafe was careful as he moved a few inches at a time.

"I've got it!" she yelled triumphantly. "I'm going to toss what I can reach to the ground." Not only did she knock down the three he'd been trying to get, but a few more tumbled down with them.

"Fantastic!"

"Thank you. Now get me down."

"Yes, ma'am." Rafe made the mistake of looking up. He had a direct view of a dainty pair of panties. His cock jumped to attention and he lost his hold on her ankles.

India let out a yelp as her grip slipped on the tree.

Thinking quick, Rafe held out his arms to catch her. She barreled into him, knocking him to the ground. He was temporarily robbed of breath.

"Oh my God!" She scrambled to her knees. "Are you all right?" Concern was etched on her lovely face.

It took a moment to get his breathing under control. The way she leaned over him made her breasts look like they'd fall out of her sundress. They hadn't been on the island for a full day, but he knew he couldn't go another second without tasting those soft looking lips.

Rafe didn't bother to give it another thought. He wrapped his arms around her waist, pulling India against him, and then rolled on top of her.

"Rafe!" she gasped in apparent surprise. "What are you doing?"

"Something I've wanted to do from the moment I laid eyes on you." His hold tightened. There was no way he'd let her go. He was so fucking hard he felt like he'd burst.

She shook her head back and forth. "No, Rafe. This isn't right. We shouldn't do this." Her protest sounded weak, and she didn't fool him for a second. India was attracted to him as much as he was to her. He'd noticed the way her gaze had cut to him earlier and how she looked at him. Even now, her body was warm and welcoming beneath his, her lips quivering as though anticipating his kiss.

Unable to deny himself a moment longer, Rafe lowered his head.

Chapter Five

The second his lips touched hers, India was utterly and completely lost. Was there any point in protesting when this was what she'd been thinking about since she met him? Rafe was right. She did want him.

His mouth was warm and insistent, pressing against hers in a hungry act of stark possession. Her hands snaked along the curve of his broad back to rest on the sides of his sinewy shoulders. She wished he weren't wearing a shirt. India wanted to feel his bare skin beneath her fingertips.

"Open your mouth. Let me taste you," he muttered against her lips as his fingers delved into her hair.

India sighed, parting her lips to grant him access, giving way for his tongue to slide and explore the recesses of her mouth. He tasted of salt—and pure heat. Her body tightened in her need and want of him. She couldn't recall craving something this deeply in a very long time, never realizing a kiss could be so powerful. Perhaps she had and that's why she'd been wary when they met. But none of that mattered now.

She clung to him and arched her body into his. Shyly, she pressed her tongue forward to meet his, and to sample all he had to offer. She tasted and circled his tongue until she was so hot she couldn't keep still.

Tearing her mouth from his, she groaned, "Rafe, we shouldn't be doing this."

"Yes, we should." He placed a hot, open-mouthed kiss on her jaw.

Her body shivered in delight. "What are you doing to me?"

"Turning you on. The same thing you're doing to me."

"But, we can't..."

"You're starting to sound like a broken record. Why are you arguing, when your body tells both of us otherwise?" Rafe unthreaded his fingers from her hair and cupped the sides of her breasts as he planted kisses against her chin and the curve of her neck. "Mmm, you have no idea what it was like to sleep next to you last night with your ass pressed against my dick. You're one sexy lady." He pulled away just enough to cover her quivering mounds with large muscular hands.

India shook in reaction. Pinpricks of pleasure raced along her spine. She wanted to denounce him, tell him she didn't want this, but she couldn't get the words past the lump in her throat.

"Tell me you weren't feeling something too."

She shook her head. "I...no." The words sounded false even to her ears.

His lips slanted into a wicked smile that made her heart flip. His amber eyes flashed with lust and blatant desire. "Liar."

India's mind was too hazy with passion to protest when he lowered the bodice of her dress. Her nipples puckered the instant the gentle island breeze brushed across them.

"Beautiful." His gaze fastened on the proud peaks.

"You only have to say one word and I'll stop right now."

Her mouth opened but nothing came out. Damn him for making her feel this way, but who was she kidding? She did want this. Boldly, she pulled him to her with a moan, loving it when his lips latched on to one of the hardened nubs, sucking it and creating a tugging motion that triggered twinges of fire between her thighs.

Rafe took his time licking and laving the tip, circling the areola until she was trembling with delight and her need to be one with him.

Suddenly, India had the strangest sensation of being watched. Turning her head slightly, she stiffened when she encountered a pair of crystal blue eyes staring back. It was like a bucket of ice water being thrown over her head.

Rafe lifted his head. "What's the matter?"

"Get off." She pushed at his shoulders, mortified at what she'd just done. India barely knew the man, yet here she was rolling in the sand with him like she was in the Chris Isaac's "Wicked Game" video. If her parents could see her now, they'd call her a whore.

Grant didn't turn away as most people probably would have in an instance like this, but then again, he was probably as shocked as she was.

Rafe happened to turn his gaze in the direction of hers and must have noticed Grant as well. "It's okay, he's—"

"No, it's not okay. Now get up!" She wiggled from beneath him, frantically tugging up the top half of her dress.

"Wait, India."

"Rafe, I said no." She scrambled to her feet and ran toward the shelter of the cave, not stopping until she was in the shaded cavern. Pressing her back against the stone wall, India slid down until her bottom hit the ground. She drew her knees to her chest. What the hell had gotten into her? Never in her life had she acted so impulsively. She was a woman of reason and logic, not some prepubescent teen who reacted solely on raging hormones.

India dropped her head against her knees, trying to banish the image of what just happened with Rafe. Her emotions were out of whack, yet the tears wouldn't come. She'd probably used them all the night before when she'd landed on this place.

The look on Grant's face only added to her humiliation. His expression was one of such abject fascination, making her wonder exactly how much he'd witnessed. It didn't seem as if he'd been disgusted or distressed at what he'd seen. He seemed as though... No. That wasn't possible. There was already too much for her to cope with. The very idea of Grant enjoying what he saw made everything even more sordid. Worst of all, why did she feel like she'd betrayed Grant by kissing Rafe?

How could she face either of them? India didn't have long to ponder the question before she was joined.

"India?" a concerned voice called out to her. It was Grant.

"Go away. I don't want to talk."

He stepped further into the cave. "I can understand—"

"I said I didn't want to talk! Please respect my wish to be alone and go away. I think I've humiliated myself enough for one day as it is. Did you come in here to see if you could get a little something of what I gave Rafe? Because if you did, you can just forget about it!"

He didn't respond for a moment and after a while she wondered if he'd left her as she'd requested, but when she lifted her head and saw him still standing there, her anger grew. "Are you deaf? I said go!" The scream reverberated through the cave creating an echo that bounced off the dank walls.

He sighed. "Fine. I'll leave, but I only wanted to make sure you're okay and to let you know I've found a fresh water source. Rafe and I will probably attempt a fire later, but because there's some nasty looking clouds forming, it makes sense if we do it in here. When you're ready, I'll show you where the water is. It's about a quarter mile inland."

India looked away from Grant, not liking how the sun cast his body in a powerful silhouette. She didn't want to notice how tall or toned his physique was, and that's exactly why he had to go. What was wrong with her? India didn't consider herself promiscuous; hell, her relationship with Steven had practically been celibate. Heavy petting and deep kissing had been as far as her ex-fiancé allowed things to go—the rat.

Before him, she'd had two lovers. One in college who'd initiated her in the carnal act. It was nice, but there had been no fireworks or sparks. Overall, it hadn't been anything to write home about. The next was Kevin, her first love. She'd met him in law school. He was suave, charming, sweet and considerate, and had taught her what the hype about sex was. Kevin was the epitome of the total package, or so she thought, until she brought him home to meet her parents.

Instead of focusing on his accomplishments and where he was going, they had zeroed in on where Kevin had been. They'd smiled in his face and pretended he was welcome in their home, but the minute he was gone, they were on her case.

"You have some nerve to bring that 'homeboy' into our house," Trevor Powers had barked.

India was floored. "I thought you liked him. You even complimented him on the brand of wine he brought. You seemed happy enough to drink it," she argued.

"Don't you dare take that tone with me, young lady! That boy is from the projects. Bed-Sty? Really, India, you might as well have brought a convict here."

"But he isn't a convict. He's a law student and he graduated summa cum laude in his class at Georgetown. If anything, he should be commended for pulling himself up by

61

the bootstraps." India knew her parents were incurable snobs, but she couldn't believe she was hearing this.

"India." Her mother had patted India on the shoulder and spoke in that condescending tone that made her shudder. "You can take the boy out of the ghetto, but you can't take the ghetto out of the boy. I won't see you married to some 'around the way' boy."

From there, her parents went on to dissect the way Kevin spoke to the way he cut his meat. By the end of the conversation, it was made plain Kevin was not welcome in their home nor would she be as long as she dated him against their wishes. Years of trying to please them had conditioned India to do exactly what they wanted.

India had ended her relationship with a bewildered Kevin and had broken her own heart in the process. She'd never forgiven herself for caving like that. She saw Kevin years later. He was just starting his own law practice and was engaged to be married. Seeing him so happy was like a punch in the stomach, not that she bore him any ill will. He deserved only the best. She'd been the one who'd behaved badly. It was her just desserts. It took some time, and she finally got over losing him, but it still nagged her when she reminded herself of all the big butthead decisions she'd made in life.

Making out with Rafe was one of them.

India realized she'd have to leave the cave eventually and deal with the repercussion of her actions, but not yet. Getting involved with either man was going to be a colossal mistake.

"What the hell happened with you two?" Grant demanded when he made his way back to his friend.

Rafe uncurled himself from the coconut tree he'd been leaning against. "I already feel like an oversized prison asshole. I don't need any more shit from you."

Grant wouldn't be dismissed so easily. "I know we talked about getting to know her a little better when we were at the airport, but I didn't think you'd end up mauling her the moment my back was turned. Shit, man, the poor woman was mortified with what she'd done."

Rafe turned on him then, his amber eyes blazing with anger. "Don't you think I realize what I've done? I didn't set out to seduce her. It just happened. She was helping me shake coconuts from the tree. I was holding her up and she fell on top of me. The next thing I knew..."

"You were all over each other?" Grant shouldn't have been jealous. This was his best friend, after all, but all those old insecurities came rearing their head once again. "I guess she prefers you then."

Rafe raked his fingers through his hair with an exasperated sigh. "It wasn't like that. I had no intention of touching her, but when our bodies touched, I lost control. I should have ignored my impulses, but I couldn't. But don't let her fool you. She wanted it just as bad as I did."

Grant snorted. "Just like Angie wanted you?"

"Let's not go down that road again. If it makes you feel any better, I won't touch her again."

Grant raised a brow in surprise. "Really?"

"It would be difficult, but I'll leave her alone."

Grant shook his head, realizing he was overreacting. How could he blame Rafe for something he himself wanted to do? "Forget it. I'm being a jackass. I saw the two of you together and got jealous."

"Because you wanted her too?"

"Of course. What hot-blooded man wouldn't want a gorgeous lady like India? It's no secret I find her attractive. No, that's an understatement. She's one of the sexiest damn women I've met in a long time. I felt a connection with her when we talked." Grant shrugged. "Guess it was wishful thinking on my part."

"Don't second-guess yourself. There could have been."

"I'm not sure. Not that it really matters. I'm sure a search team will be sent out to rescue us, so the point is moot."

"But in the eventuality we're not?"

The last thing Grant wanted to think about was being on this island longer than a day or two, but the possibility was too real to ignore. "We'll cross that bridge when we come to it. In the meantime, we'll focus on staying alive."

Rafe grabbed his arm when he would have walked on. "And what about India? We can't continue this charade that there's nothing happening between us, and I'm not just talking about me and her. I mean all of us."

"The decision will have to be hers. Come on. Let me show you the fresh water source I found." Grant was eager to end this conversation, because a far worse possibility than staying on the island, was discovering India wasn't as interested in him as she was Rafe.

Chapter Six

Three more restless days and sleepless nights had passed with no sign of a rescue team in sight. It was starting to sink in with them all that maybe they wouldn't be getting off the island anytime soon. The very thought terrified her. All they'd had to eat so far were coconuts and a crab that had washed up on the shore. The water source was swarming with insects, but it was either drink or die of thirst.

Rafe and Grant were unable to get a fire started, sleeping on the cold hard ground made her muscles stiff, and the bugs were eating her alive. The weather went from one extreme to the next. When it wasn't scorching hot, it was raining, and the nights were freezing. She had no choice but to sleep huddled between Rafe and Grant for body heat.

Being on this island was tantamount to Hell.

None of them spoke of the incident between her and Rafe, but it was obvious from the way they were so painfully polite to each other that it still preyed on their minds. She could also tell by the fact they were going out of their way to put her at ease. No matter how they chose to ignore the tension, it remained beneath the surface, simmering, waiting to boil over.

India wasn't sure if she would be able to take it anymore. She'd had three days to come to terms with what she'd done, and it was silly to act as if it didn't happen. Besides, for all she knew they could be on this island forever. It made no sense to tiptoe around anyone's sensibilities this long. India shivered under the icy curtain of the water raining over her head and gliding down her body.

She would have given anything to be home standing under a nice steamy shower, but this had to do for now. Anyway, it was pretty lucky that Grant had found this waterfall. Were they not in such a dire situation, she would have appreciated the surroundings of this tropical paradise a little more, from the wild vegetation, to the exotic birds of all colors of the rainbow, to the crystal water hitting white sand. It could have been on a postcard. Too bad she didn't want to be here.

When India couldn't stand beneath the forceful spray any longer, she waded out of the water and wrung out her hair with a grimace. Without any hair care products, a blow dryer or flat iron, she'd been sporting an afro. Since there were no mirrors either, she'd been spared the sight she must have made.

India thanked her lucky stars she'd just received her regular Depo-Provera shot before coming on this vacation. One of the side effects of the birth control method was her lack of a period. She winced to think of dealing with that out here without the proper equipment, and prayed they'd be rescued before it wore out in three months.

She silently cursed as she pulled her dress back on. One of the straps had torn on a twig and the bodice was already ripped in the front, dipping low enough to give anyone who looked a show. Why hadn't she worn something more practical during her trip, instead of this flimsy piece of cotton? She didn't even have the benefit of a bra since her sundress was the kind that had one already built in.

Besides a pair of lacy bikini panty briefs, India felt completely exposed. But on the flipside, she wondered what

Rafe and Grant thought of her. Did they sometimes find themselves stealing glances at her, surveying her every curve as she did with them. Ludicrous as it was, she couldn't help thinking about Rafe and what he'd done to her body and what would have happened if Grant had done more than watch?

She shook her head, banishing the thought from her mind, then finished dressing, adjusting her dress to cover as much skin as possible. With a deep breath, she squared her shoulders and headed back to camp, prepared to face the men. The moment she stepped onto the beach, she heard shouts and yelling. What was going on? Was everything okay? Was one of the men hurt?

India ran toward the commotion without another thought, hoping for the best, but expecting the worst. The sight which greeted her, however, was of Rafe and Grant dancing around and hugging each other like a couple of lunatics in their apparent jubilation.

Did they spot a plane? Cautiously, she walked over to them. Grant spotted her first and ran over to her. Before India could protest, he lifted her in the air, swinging her around until she pushed his shoulders. "Have you lost your mind? Put me down!" She smacked him on the chest.

Grant laughed, unperturbed, slowly lowering her along the length of his hard body. She felt every ripple and every hollow of his taut form. She couldn't stop the gasp from escaping her lips at being made aware of his blatant masculinity. Pulling out of his arms, she took a step back. "What's going on? And why are you two acting like you won the lottery?"

"Look!" Rafe pointed toward their cave and India noticed for the first time puffs of white smoke billowing out.

"Fire?" She'd known how frustrated the two men had been over not being able to start one, and now that they had, and realizing how much it meant to their survival, she threw her head back and whooped at their triumph. "This is great! Thank God, we won't damn near freeze to death another night and if we ever catch a fish or another crab, we'll have a way to cook it. How did you finally do it?"

Grant grinned, pride etching the corners of his eyes. "A lot of hard work. We realized the sticks weren't catching fire no matter how much we rubbed them together. Then Rafe got the idea of using the coconut husk and viola! Actually, it took some time, but we finally got that sucker started. Now we simply have to figure out how to keep it going."

"I suggest we collect as much wood and flammable objects as possible to burn so we'll have a surplus, and it will be all of our responsibilities to watch it." Rafe slipped his hands in his pockets.

India nodded. "Or we can take shifts. Whatever you guys decide, I'll go along with it." She silently counted to ten before making her next statement, knowing if she didn't bring the subject up now she'd lose her nerve. "Guys, I...uh, think we need to talk." The statement hung in the air between them and for a moment, she didn't think either one of them would respond.

Finally, Rafe answered. "Yes, I think we should too. It looks like it's going to rain. We should probably take shelter."

She followed them inside and stilled when she got a good look inside the cave. The fire illuminated the place and she saw things she hadn't noticed before. In the corner of the cave was a large set of animal bones and it freaked her out. "What is that?" India pointed to the fossil.

Grant shrugged. "It could have been a wild boar or something similar, judging from the shape and size."

"I knew there was the possibility of animals roaming the

island, but I didn't think they'd dwell this far from the forest."
So much had happened in the past few days that the idea
hadn't crossed her mind. It meant their shelter wasn't as safe
as she'd assumed, yet another reason it sucked to be stuck on a
deserted island.

"If there are, they're probably further inland." Grant patted
her shoulder. His words were meant to reassure her, but they
didn't help. She hoped she didn't run into a wild beast.

She took a seat in front of the fire, watching the orange
embers dance. A lump formed in her throat while she tried to
gather the right words to say. There was no point in beating
around the bush. "Look, we can't pretend the incident between
Rafe and I didn't happen. We've all been skirting around the
subject and I know it's my fault." India nibbled her bottom lip.
"And I'm sorry it happened." There. It was out in the open.

"I think the craziness of the past few days sort of went to
my head. I needed that kiss as some kind of validation that I
was alive, to feel something other than the despair and
frustration of being stranded here."

A ferocious scowl marred Rafe's rugged features. "It was
more than a kiss and you know it. If this is confession time,
then at least tell the truth."

His accusation hit her like a smack in the face.
"What...what do you mean? I am telling the truth."

Rafe lifted a dark sinister brow. "Oh? Why not admit how
you wiggled and squirmed beneath me, pressing your body
against mine? You wanted more than to just prove your were
alive. You were attracted to me."

"Stop it," she whispered.

"Rafe." Grant spoke his name in a soft rejoinder.

Rafe wouldn't be stopped. "No. I've held my tongue long
enough. Go ahead, India. Tell us how you moaned my name

and clung to me like you were burning for it."

Her mouth flew open and her cheeks burned in embarrassment. What could she say to that when what he said was true? She had wanted him. Badly. But to say the words aloud would change the dynamics between them forever. "It's this situation. I'm not that kind of woman."

"You were the other day," Rafe taunted.

India's gaze cut to Grant to gauge his reaction and to beg his assistance. Why was he sitting there not saying anything? "Grant?"

Rafe reached over and grabbed her wrist. "Tell us the truth, India. You wanted me as more than just a convenient man to validate your existence. I'm beginning to think the only reason you're upset is because we were caught. Did you like Grant watching us? Is that it? Does voyeurism turn you on?"

"Don't be disgusting!" She yanked her wrist from his grip and covered her ears with her hands.

"Rafe, that's enough. She's not ready for this."

India did hear that. She dropped her hands, turning her gaze in the blond's direction. "What are you talking about? What am I not ready for?"

The men looked at each other silently, not saying a word, but it seemed like they knew what the other was thinking.

Rafe finally broke the uncomfortable silence. "I'm sorry, India. I didn't mean to hammer this topic so hard, but I can't let you pretend you didn't want what happened as much as I did. Furthermore, there's no point in hiding your attraction to Grant."

"That isn't...I'm..." She closed her mouth, unable to form the words on her lips. Anger surged through her. She clenched her fists at her side. "Are the two of you thinking of having some sick threesome? Is that what this is all about?"

"You're the one who wanted to talk, India. If we're getting our feelings out in the open, I think it should all be laid on the table," Rafe challenged.

She scrambled to her feet, unwilling to listen to any more. "Do you think I'm a slut? You must, if you think I'm the type to go for something like that. I'm sorry I started this conversation, but the two of you can go to hell if you think I'll allow either one of you to touch me!" She strode toward the cave entrance.

Grant called out, "Where are you going? It's pouring out there."

"I'd rather be in the storm than deal with the two of you right now." She, walked out into the rain. It beat against her skin, stinging her like angry wasps. It barely registered, however, as she continued to walk along the shoreline. The weather was easier to deal with than the reality of Rafe's accusations. It wouldn't have bothered her so much if it weren't true.

"What the fuck is wrong with you? Did you have to come on so strong?" Grant looked as if he wanted to punch him, but Rafe knew he wouldn't.

Even if his friend did strike him, Rafe wasn't prepared to back down. "I'm sorry she's upset, but I'm not sorry I said it. It needed to be brought out in the open. Things have been so damn tense it's stifling the hell out of me, and I for one wasn't going to carry on this game of make-believe that nothing happened. Now that I've had a taste of her, I can't go back and I don't think you can either."

"I have nothing to go back to. You're the one she prefers."

"Give me a break! I wish you wouldn't start that shit again. Of course she's interested in you too; why do you think she's having such a hard time dealing with what I said. If it wasn't true, she would have taken my comments in stride, but instead, India freaked out."

"Maybe because it isn't."

"No. Because it is. I'm one hundred percent certain. I'm not blind to the way she's been staring at either one of us. You're a fool if you haven't noticed it. You're just pissed because you didn't get to her first."

A furious blush of red colored Grant's cheeks, and Rafe knew his point had hit home. "Goddammit, you could have given her some time to get used to us a little more. Perhaps she might have been more receptive to the possibility of exploring our lifestyle, but you blew it because you couldn't stop thinking with your cock!" Grant glared, his lips thinning to one angry line.

Rafe rolled his eyes. "It may have been okay for the two of you to continue this pantomime of politeness, but this won't wash for long. We're going to have to face the fact that we may be stuck on this island for a long time—if not for the rest of our lives. I, for one, can't spend the rest of my days with my dick in a sling. I want her, you want her, and she can deny it all she pleases, but India wants us too!"

Grant's nostrils flared as he crossed his arms. "Tell me, Rafe, do you actually care about her or is she just convenient pussy for you?"

Rafe paused. Would they be having this conversation had India not been the only female survivor on the island? Part of his agreement with Grant about sharing a woman was finding someone they could both love, and who would love them back equally. Angie had shown him that the sex could be good when he shared with his best friend, but it wouldn't be fulfilling if feelings weren't involved, and Rafe was long past the point in life where a meaningless fuck was all he wanted from a woman.

"Honestly," he finally answered, "no. She's gorgeous, and God knows it's hard not to stare at her and not be blown away, but it's much more than that. That's why I'm so desperate to be with her. When I met her at the airport, I saw a sadness in her eyes and I wanted to banish it. And then we spoke and I wanted to know more about her. I sense in her something special. You know how it is when you meet someone and you feel a certain connection with them?"

Grant nodded slowly. "Sort of like when we met."

"Exactly like that. The last time I felt such a strong connection with another person was with you. We met, I didn't think there would ever be someone who cared about me, and whom I could care for in return. You came into my life at a time when I didn't feel like I was worth shit. We couldn't have predicted this plane crash, but I feel that India is here for a reason, and I'm not going to lose the possibility of the three of us coming together because of her misguided moral dilemma. You shared that same spark when you met her, didn't you?"

Grant sighed, uncrossing his arms. "Yes. I knew she'd be special, though I didn't know fate would kick us in the nuts by throwing the three of us on this island. It's almost like we were meant to be together. But..." He shook his head. "It doesn't necessarily mean she'll get on board with our plans, just because we're horny."

"It's much more than that and you know it."

"I do know, but that's what she may think. For all she knows, we could be just a couple of perverts trying to get our rocks off. Hell, before the Angie debacle, I may have been inclined to agree with her."

Rafe stood up from the uncomfortable sitting position he'd been in. "I see no point in dancing around the issue, and I'm glad she knows the deal."

Grant stood up as well. "And exactly what should we say to her? India, since we're all attracted to each other, let's fuck?"

"Why not?"

"Because it's crude! These things take finesse. Besides, she's already suffered enough."

"And we haven't? I'm tired of going to sleep wondering where our next meal will come from, not having a hot shower, a proper shave, a pillow to rest beneath my head, a cold beer— you know, the things we once took for granted. I don't want my only thoughts to be of whether or not I'm going to die on this godforsaken island. The despair and loss of hope could kill a man out here. I want to experience something other than that emotion. I want to feel…"

"Lust?"

"Yes! And passion. Tell me I'm wrong if you want, but I know you well enough to realize you want the same thing. I'm just not going to be a hypocrite about it." Rafe strode toward the cave entrance with every intention of getting India back.

"Wait!" Grant gripped his shoulder.

Rafe turned around, wariness settling over him. He was through with arguing about this. It was time for action.

"I'll come with you."

Rafe gave his friend a long, assessing look, seeing the resignation in Grant's eyes. He couldn't fault Grant's sensitivity for other people's feelings; it was one of the qualities he'd admired most about him, but now wasn't the time to play the chivalrous knight. "Okay." He nodded. "Let's go get our woman."

Chapter Seven

India shivered beneath the cold, sharp rain tearing into her skin. She didn't know how long she'd walked or in what direction she'd been going, but she ended up in an unfamiliar stretch of woods. Since they'd been here, India hadn't familiarized herself with the island as much as she should have, preferring to stay close to the cave and the waterfall when she needed to wash. Now she had no idea where she was and darkness was near.

Maybe she'd die out here and it would be all Rafe and Grant's fault! They'd placed her in this predicament. Had they not confronted her with their perversions...no, that wasn't exactly true. It had been Rafe. From the beginning she knew he was the aggressive go-getter type who went after what he wanted. The kind of attitude most women found sexy as hell, but for him to say what he did was not right.

The cutting part however, was the fact that Grant had sat by and not done anything, defended her. He was the one she felt the deeper emotional bond with. Why didn't he speak up? It was useless in answering that question. He was no better than Rafe. They both wanted to treat her like some two-bit streetwalker.

India wouldn't allow them to use her for their amusement, not even if they weren't ever rescued. What they wanted was dirty...and wrong. Now if she only could figure out where she was... It wouldn't be so bad if the rain didn't make visibility so low. She wandered a few more yards before she stumbled, falling face first into a puddle of mud.

"I won't cry," she muttered with determination, dragging herself to a sitting position. Her resolve was shattered seconds later as a cry escaped her lips. Sobs racked her body, her tears mingling with the rain. She hadn't cried since that first night when they buried that body, and now that was all she could think to do. India couldn't recall giving in to her emotions this way ever. This island was bringing out the worst in her and the feelings of helplessness didn't sit well with her.

Even the years of parental neglect, teasing in school and realizing she'd never be the person most people expected her to be, had never made her break down like this. India wished she hadn't allowed her anger to take her out of the cave and into unfamiliar territory. She sat unmoving for several moments waiting for something, anything to happen, when the rain stopped abruptly, not steadily easing up as it usually did.

Now she should be able to find her way back. How big could this place be exactly? India fought to stand, her legs weak and tired. She couldn't remember being this bone weary since studying without sleep for the bar exam. Wandering through the forest, India looked for landmarks she may have seen before, but didn't see anything she recognized.

Just when she was ready to give up, she halted upon hearing her name called out. "India!" The sound was faint, but it was there.

"I'm here!" She tried to yell, but it came out as a weak croak.

"India!" The voices were getting closer.

She cleared her throat before calling out again. "Here I am!"

India moved toward the sound of her name until the rustling of footsteps greeted her ears.

Rafe was the first one she saw, followed by Grant. She was so relieved to see them, India nearly threw herself into their arms, but memories of their last conversation had her staying where she stood.

"Thank goodness you're okay." Rafe's relief was evident.

She wasn't about to let them see how scared she'd been. "What? Didn't you two think I could take care of myself? I'm not some helpless damsel in distress, you know." They didn't need to know she'd been lost. India had conceded too much to them already.

"What were you doing all the way out here?" Grant asked, looking around, a worried expression crinkling his forehead.

"I needed to think." India didn't bother elaborating.

"Let's go back to the cave. It's getting dark and you need to warm yourself by the fire. You're soaked." Rafe reached out to take her hand, but she pulled back.

"Don't touch me."

Rafe took a step closer. "India, why are you fighting this so hard? Didn't you realize it was inevitable the three of us would eventually be together?"

India took two steps back. "I don't want to hear this."

Amber eyes flashed fire. "That's too damn bad because you're going to listen."

"Kiss my ass." She turned on her heel, but was immediately yanked around to face a visibly angry Rafe. "Your ass isn't the only thing I want to kiss and you know it!"

Unable to control the ire building within her, she balled her fingers into a fist and swung at him.

Rafe caught her wrist in his hand before her punch

connected. She attempted to slap him with her free hand, but was again thwarted. "Would you stop it, India?"

"No! I won't stop it, because I don't want this!" She swung her gaze in Grant's direction. "Are you going to stand there and let this happen? If you do, you're just as bad as he is."

Grant shook his head. "Rafe, let her go."

Rafe's expression grew even stormier. "Hell no. We talked about this; you agreed—"

"I agreed the attraction was mutual between India and us. I came with you so you wouldn't try anything crazy. India..." Grant walked closer to them, "...you may not want to hear this, but from the moment we saw you, we realized there was something happening between us. This is by no means a conventional situation, nor do we expect you to fall into our plans so easily, but to deny you're not at least curious about exploring the possibilities of being with the two of us is a lie. You don't strike me as a person to speak untruths."

Grant's soft-spoken words hit their mark where Rafe's forceful tactics had failed.

"I don't want it to be true," she whispered, thinking herself as depraved as Rafe and Grant to even entertain what they were suggesting.

"Wanting it to go away won't make it happen, but you'll feel better if you admit how you feel." Grant brushed a stray lock of wet hair from her forehead.

She lowered her lids, unable to meet his probing blue gaze. "I...I am attracted to the both of you, but...I don't think I can handle something like this. It's wrong."

"According to whom? The rules are created by people who don't practice what they preach. The hypocrisy is sickening. Why is it wrong—if it makes the people involved happy, and isn't hurting anyone else? Something like this can't be denied,"

Rafe insisted. He released her wrists and hauled her against the hard wall of his chest, squeezing her against him before letting her go, just enough to give him space to cup her breasts.

India groaned as Rafe grazed her nipples with his thumbs. She should stop him, but it was difficult to think when he touched her this way. Grant moved behind her and placed calloused hands on her shoulders before lowering his hand and pressing a kiss on the nape of her neck.

"Please don't." It wasn't much of a protest because even now she pushed her bottom against Grant's crotch. His erection pressed against her. In the back of her mind, India thought of how wrong this was, yet like they'd both said, this moment was inevitable.

Rafe rubbed and kneaded her breasts, shaping them in his large palms. "Don't you see how good it can be between us?"

No longer could she pretend this wasn't what she'd fantasized about since she'd seen these two hunks. Right now she wanted to throw caution to the wind and do something wicked and wild. They were right. The only person she'd been fooling about her lust for them was herself.

Grant pulled her away from Rafe and turned her around to face him. Not giving her a chance to blink, his mouth crushed her lips, savaging her. The four day growth of whiskers tickled her skin, but she loved the rough sensation of it grazing her face. India's response to him was instant. She didn't think she could be so thoroughly aroused by two men at once in her life.

India grasped Grant's shoulders, clinging to him, wanting his kiss as much as the air she breathed. His questing hands slid down her back to rest on her ass. He molded his cock against her pelvis.

Grant broke the kiss and pressed his forehead against hers, his breathing ragged. "Jesus, India. You have no idea how much I've wanted to do that."

"I didn't know how much I wanted you to do that to me until now," she answered honestly. She backed away from him, putting some distance between her and the two men, eyeing them both and trying to come to grips with what she was about to do with them. She moistened her lips with the tip of her tongue. "I...I don't want you two to think this is something I normally do, but under these circumstances..."

Rafe shook his head. "You've admitted you want us, that's the first step, but let's not backtrack by making believe this wouldn't have happened under any circumstance. The attraction is too strong for us to say otherwise. Let's go back to the cave and get warm together." He gently took her hand in his and Grant took the other.

India shut her eyes for a brief moment. This was it.

Grant was anxious as they drew closer to the cave. He could tell India was nervous from the way she shook. He squeezed her hand in reassurance, giving her a smile of encouragement. She was so beautiful and he couldn't believe they would finally have this ebony goddess just as Rafe said they would. In a way, he was glad Rafe had pushed the issue, otherwise they may have still been skirting around it, but he wondered if she was simply giving in to them because she felt she had no choice. As much as he wanted nothing more than to take her on the ground and fuck her senseless, he needed to make sure one last time that she was ready to accept both of them as her lovers.

He stopped just before they entered their shelter. Grant turned to her. "Is this what you want?"

India hesitated for only a second. "Yes. I do want this. I don't know why I was fighting the inevitable so hard. You and Rafe were right, this was meant to be."

Relief flooded his chest. Grant didn't know what he would have done if she'd changed her mind. His cock was straining painfully against his pants, and right now all he could think about was driving into her tight sheath.

"Then what the hell are we waiting for," Rafe growled, propelling her forward. Once inside, Rafe grabbed India to him and placed an urgent kiss against the curve of her elegant throat.

Grant refused to be a spectator on the sidelines. Moving behind her, he cupped her shoulders, reveling in the silky smoothness of her mocha skin. He pushed her straps down before raining kisses over the exposed flesh.

India groaned against Rafe's mouth and then hooked an arm around Grant's waist. She wiggled her bottom against his cock, making Grant's throbbing more painful than before. He needed her.

"So beautiful," he murmured against her skin, raising her dress to run his fingers between her thighs. Already she was wet and ready.

"Oh," she sighed, resting the back of her head against the crook of his shoulder.

Grant slipped his fingers inside her panties, encountering a soft patch of curly hair between the juncture of her thighs. "You're so warm," he murmured, pleased at her arousal.

He noticed Rafe reaching into her bodice and freeing her full breasts.

"Perfect. I haven't been able to get these lovelies out of my mind since I last had the pleasure of tasting them the first time. By the way you're squirming for it, you want my mouth on you.

Don't you, India?"

"Yes," she groaned.

A smile curled the corners of Grant's lips. There was something arousing about seeing Rafe and India interact. If she was turned on now, Grant planned on turning up the heat several more notches.

Grant dropped to his knees behind her, taking his hands from inside of her panties. "Part your thighs for me, darling," he commanded softly, prying her legs apart a little further.

India complied, wiggling her delectable backside in the process. Grant wanted no barriers between them. Grabbing the edge of her panties, he pulled them down her shapely thighs and legs, admiring how supple and soft she was. He couldn't help running his hands along her rear and down the backs of her thighs. Even the contrast of his pale hand against her dark skin was an arousing sight.

Helping her step out of her panties, one foot at a time, Grant tossed them aside, careful not to throw them too close to the flame.

The soft mewling sounds she made in the back of her throat were driving him crazy. Grant stole a brief glance up at India to see her dig her fingers into Rafe's dark hair as he suckled one taut nipple, before returning to his task.

"Good God, you're wet," Grant whispered in wonder upon seeing the trail of moisture drip from her pussy. Placing his head between her thighs, Grant licked at the stream of moisture, savoring the tangy flavor on his tongue. "Delicious," he murmured, before planting kisses on her ass and inside of her legs.

"Grant," she groaned, practically shoving her rear in his face. Parting her damp labia, he found her throbbing clit slick with her juices. He rolled the hot bud between his thumb and forefinger, applying pressure and then releasing.

"Do you like that, India?"

Grant already knew the answer to that question from the way she moved against him, silently begging for it, but he wanted to hear her vocalize the affirmative.

"Yes! Oh, yes!" Her shout of ecstasy served to increase his arousal. He shoved a middle finger into her slick channel. Shit, she was tight. Grant could only begin to imagine how it would feel to have his cock buried in her cunt, gripping him like a vise.

Squirming her bottom, she moved with him as he fingered her.

"That's it, darling. Don't hold back. Give me everything you've got."

"Rafe...Grant. This feels so good. Ah!" she cried out.

Grant slipped another finger into her pussy, stretching her for his cock. He wasn't a small man and neither was Rafe. With a pussy this tight, he'd have to prepare her first. He squeezed her luscious ass with his free hand before giving it a playful smack.

"Oh!" Her momentary gasp of surprise became a satisfied purr. He couldn't take it anymore. Grant had to be inside of her now. Slowly, he eased his fingers from her damp channel and brought them to his mouth, slurping every bit of her essence from his skin. Grant couldn't remember the last time he'd been this aroused and he could barely contain himself.

He was so eager for her, his hands were trembling almost like his first time with Susie Jordano in her parents' bedroom. Only this time there was no rush or fear of her father coming home to bust them. And this moment was definitely more special because he and his best friend were pleasuring a very desirable woman who turned him on in ways no words could describe.

He pulled back just enough to tug his polo shirt over his head and then he undid his pants and removed his boxers in a hurry. Grant's dick throbbed, bright red with his desire.

"I need to be inside of you now, darling. I don't think I can hold on much longer."

Rafe lifted his head, letting go of her nipple with a wet slurp. Grant looked at the other man and his friend nodded in their silent communication.

"Look at me, sweetheart," Grant commanded.

India did as she was told, her breath coming out in hurried gasps, her body trembling in her passion. "What do you want me to do?"

Grant reached up to tug her dress all the way off. "I want you on your knees so I can fuck you."

Chapter Eight

The moment had come. There was no turning back now. India pushed away the nagging voice in the back of her head. It told her she shouldn't be enjoying this so much, but the way Rafe had been nibbling on her breasts, teasing and tormenting the highly sensitized mounds, caused all reason to fly out the window. If that wasn't enough, the stimulation of Grant fingering her, heightened the sensation like nothing she'd ever experienced, sending an erotic charge along her nerve endings.

Rafe placed his hands on her shoulders, gently guiding her down to the ground. She trembled in uncertainty and pleasure combined.

"Don't be frightened, India. We wouldn't do anything to hurt you," Grant whispered in her ear and then tugged her lobe with his teeth. He reached around to cup her breasts. "You have a beautiful body, darling. You have no idea how long I've wanted to do this."

Rafe lowered himself in front of her as he tugged his shirt off to reveal the golden muscular expanse of his hard chest, dusted with a dark mat of hair. India had to touch him. Placing her hands on his torso, she massaged his flesh.

"Your body is so tight," she said with frank admiration.

Rafe released a throaty moan, closing his amber eyes, masking the desire lurking within their depths.

She dragged her fingers across his nipples and leaned forward, pressing a kiss against his pecs. Rafe trembled beneath the light touch of her lips.

Grant was making it difficult to concentrate on her task, however, as he ran his hands over her body with liberal strokes, leaving no part of her skin unexplored.

India cried out when he pinched and tugged on her nipples. "Oh, Jesus," she muttered, digging her nails into Rafe's skin.

The urge to touch Rafe and give the pleasure she'd received from him and was still receiving from Grant drove her to undo Rafe's pants and yank them down. He helped her with his boxers and revealed a long thick cock.

Her eyes widened at the sheer length and girth. It was as big as Grant's felt, pressed against her rear. "Do you like what you see?" Rafe's voice sounded breathy, as though he were struggling to get the words out.

"Very much," she answered without hesitation.

"Then touch me. I need your hands on me."

India encircled his member with her fingers, testing its weight with her palms and giving it a light squeeze.

A throaty moan escaped his lips.

Her hand glided along his rod, tugging and pushing him gently.

Rafe's sharp intake of breath told her how turned on he was and that gave her a sense of empowerment, knowing that she could bring this hunk of a man to his knees.

Grant's warm breath against her skin sent goose bumps along her arms and the back of her neck. A fire burned between her legs and she wanted a cock inside of her—needed it.

Grinding her backside against Grant's hardness, India silently pleaded for him to take her.

"You're ready for me, aren't you?" Grant murmured against her skin at the juncture where her neck and shoulder met.

"Yes. Please. Take me."

Grant chuckled. "Don't worry, sweetheart, I have every intention of doing just that." He pulled her against him.

India wasn't sure how this was suppose to work with both of them. She looked at Rafe and then turned her head to stare at Grant. "What should I do?"

"Get on all fours, and we'll take care of the rest," Rafe instructed.

India placed her hands on the cool hard ground, a little scared and excited at the same time. She didn't pause to think about what she was doing. All she wanted to do was feel this mind-blowing pleasure.

Grant remained behind her, pushing her thighs further apart.

She stiffened when he parted her cheeks and rubbed her anus. India had only had anal sex a few times with Kevin. The experience had been pleasant if not her absolute favorite act of the carnal arts, but she certainly didn't want to have it right now without lubrication, especially with a cock the size of Grant's. "Don't. Not without..."

"Shh. It's okay, sweetheart," Grant assured. "I just want to play with you a little." He continued to glide his thumb around the tight ring until she relaxed and was soon quivering with desire.

"Why are you teasing me like this? You know what I want," she groaned, looking over her shoulder.

Bright blue eyes twinkled with lust as she met his hungry gaze. An emotion she couldn't quite name hit her with such an intense force she looked away from him, and turned her attention to Rafe.

He'd shed his pants and now he was on his knees before her, fisting his cock, a look of pure animalistic passion stamped on his face. It sent a titillating thrill along her spine.

She licked her lips. "Let me taste you."

"I thought you'd never ask." Rafe moved forward until the tip of the mushroom-shaped head was against her mouth.

Sliding her tongue along the conical tip, she circled the velvety skin.

Rafe dug his fingers in her hair. "That's it, baby. Lick it."

India sampled his cock with broad strokes, leaving no part of it unbathed with her tongue, tracing every veiny inch of him. Opening her mouth over his dick, she took a little bit of him between her lips.

Gently, Rafe pulled back and then pushed deeper until she was nearly swallowing him.

Grant stroked her with his cock, moving it along her rear, and sliding it against the cleft of her pussy, teasing and driving India to the brink of insanity. She backed up against him.

"Easy, sweetheart. I want to make this last. There's no rush," Grant whispered.

He was wrong. There was every need to rush because she thought she'd combust if he didn't put his dick in her. Whimpering with her hunger and gnawing ache for him, India nearly cried in relief when Grant finally pushed his cock into her wet passage.

"Jesus Christ!" He slowly slid into her, one delicious inch at a time, stretching and filling her so wonderfully. "So tight. Just like I knew you'd be."

India could only moan her pleasure as Rafe thrust his cock in and out of her mouth.

Grant remained still as though allowing her to adjust to his size. India however wasn't prepared for his chivalry. She wanted his big dick pumping into her.

Jerking her body back, she slammed against his pelvis, sending Grant balls deep into her. She felt like weeping at the sheer bliss of the moment. It felt so incredibly good to have him inside of her. India never thought anything could induce such nerve-jolting rapture like being fucked this way. If someone would have told her one day she'd end up with two hunks at once, one in her pussy and the other in her mouth, she wouldn't have believed them. In fact she probably would have called them crazy.

Straitlaced India Powers would never do something this wild and wanton, something so totally irresponsible, but she loved every single moment of this. And for the life of her, she couldn't figure out why she had denied them to begin with.

It took her a moment to find her rhythm, but she began to move in sync with them, almost as if they were performing a choreographed dance. She matched them thrust for thrust. India gripped their cocks with her lips and pussy, pulling them deeper into her orifices, eliciting sighs and moans from each man.

"Oh, hell yes," Rafe shouted as his fingers burrowed deeper into her hair.

Grant grasped her hips, slamming his cock into her like a man possessed, so hard it almost felt like he was hitting her womb. It hurt a bit, but it was a good kind of hurt, the point between pleasure and pain. She was filled with a primitive need to be branded by him.

"So...good...so...tight." Grant groaned the words, barely able to get them out. "You were made for my cock—for us." He pushed harder still.

An explosion burst from her very core and spread through India, rocking her entire body. She ripped her mouth away from Rafe's cock to scream her climax. She couldn't stop shaking. Her pussy gushed with cream as Grant continued to plow into her. "Grant," she moaned.

He shoved into her several more times, before pulling out. A warm spurt of liquid hit her ass. Grant shouted his release.

India turned her head to look at him. "Why did you pull out? Didn't you want to...?" Her cheeks grew warm. Despite what she'd just done with them, India couldn't bring herself to say the words on her mind.

Rafe didn't give Grant a chance to answer. "It's my turn to get some of that sweet pussy." He hauled her into his arms, their bodies mashing together.

Rafe caught her gasp in his mouth, swallowing her cry of surprise. Her mouth on his cock, though wonderful, wasn't enough. He needed all of her. India tasted of coconut, salt and pure heaven. Every time he kissed her it felt like the first time.

Everything about her sent his senses reeling from her beauty, passion and her insatiable hunger for them. Reluctantly he broke the kiss, unable to ignore his throbbing cock any longer. Seeing Grant pumping into her had fed his hunger for her, leaving him starving.

"Wrap your arms around me, India."

She moved closer, straddling his thighs and rubbing her damp pussy against his cock.

Rafe's breath caught in his throat at how good it was to have her in his arms. "That's it, baby. Now lift your hips."

She licked her lips, as she looked at him with passion-glazed eyes. "I want you."

"And you're going to have me. Every inch of me." Grabbing his cock, he rubbed the head along her slit before slipping it into her cunt. It was just as tight as he knew it would be. Like a wet satin glove, it clenched his dick, gripping and sucking him deep. Nothing felt more right than being one with her.

India buried her face in his neck with a sigh of her obvious content.

Rafe glanced over her shoulder and saw Grant slide behind India and begin to massage her back, touching his lips to her sweat-glistened skin.

A feeling Rafe couldn't explain moved through him as he drove into her, trying to go as deep as possible. It was a warmth, a sense of intimacy he had yet to experience with anyone else before. When he met Grant's gaze, Rafe knew his friend was thinking the same things. Being with India like this confirmed what they'd already suspected from the beginning.

She was their woman.

It was one thing to suppose it, but a completely different matter to know with absolute certainty. He guessed he and Grant could have shared a dozen women together, but never would have come close to experiencing the euphoria coursing through his veins at this very moment.

Rafe realized their circumstances had propelled them together, making it happen much sooner than it would have were they back in civilization. However, had they met India in a different setting, they still would have ended up together.

"Rafe," she moaned his name against his chest, her breathing hot and heavy.

"That's it, baby. Let go. Give yourself over to me."

She clasped his shoulder and threw her head back, resting it on Grant. India bounced up and down on his cock. "Yes! Yes! Yes!" she screamed.

Grant snaked his hands around her body to fondle her breasts and it seemed to take her to the edge.

India gripped Rafe's cock tighter, her pussy holding on to him and refusing to let go. He had no prayer of lasting.

More than anything, Rafe wanted to come inside of her, but that wouldn't happen until they had a frank and open discussion about where their relationship was going.

India screamed her climax, her cream oozing from her pussy in a warm gush.

When Rafe was too close to his own orgasm, he grabbed her waist and lifted her off of his dick.

Bewilderment swam within the depths of her dark brown eyes as he shot his load against her thigh. "Why did you do that?"

"Because you're not ready for it."

India frowned, but didn't press the issue.

Rafe took her hand in his. "Come on. It's dark out and we might as well get some sleep for the night. We'll talk about this in the morning."

She shook her head, pulling her hand away and scooting out of his reach. "No. We'll talk about this now, and could one of you toss my dress over to me?"

Rafe grabbed his shirt and handed it to her. "Here, try this on. I think I might have ripped the front of your dress."

She groaned before taking it. "Other than my underwear, it's the only article of clothing I have."

"Well, you're welcome to our shirts. We don't need them, or feel free to walk around naked," Grant teased.

India didn't look amused. She moved closer to the fire and put Rafe's shirt on. It looked better on her than it ever did on him. His cock grew hard at the way it crested over her gentle curves.

Silence fell between the three of them, making Rafe tense. He wondered what she had to say. Was she going to tell them this was a one time deal? If that was the case she was out of her mind. He stood up and grabbed his pants, stuffing his legs in and then yanking them up. Rafe began to pace the cave, full of nervous energy, trying to find the right words to say.

"You two have done this before, haven't you?" India finally broke the quiet.

Rafe looked at Grant, not trusting himself to speak for fear of saying the wrong thing. Grant was much better with words than him, more tactful and didn't normally blurt out the first thing on his mind.

Grant slid closer to India.

India turned away from him. "Do you mind putting your pants on, please?"

"Why? My nudity didn't bother you before when we were fucking you."

Rafe lifted a brow, surprised at his friend's response. That was something he would have said. He dipped his head slightly to hide his smile.

India didn't share his amusement. "Must you be so crude about it?" She looked into the fire, stubbornly refusing to meet either of their gazes.

"No, but neither is it necessary for you to play the vestal virgin when we all know you're anything but."

For a minute Rafe thought India would strangle Grant for that comment, but instead her shoulders sagged in defeat. "You're right. I'm acting like a prude, but I'm sure you can imagine this is a weird situation for me."

Grant nodded. "I'm sorry."

She shrugged. "It's alright. I think we've all been crazy these past few days understandably. But back to my original question: have you two done this before?"

Chapter Nine

India waited in tense anticipation for one of them to answer. Something told her that they had been with one woman simultaneously before. She could sense it from the way they looked at each other, speaking without uttering a single word. Their movements had been too practiced, too in tune with each other for it not to be the first time they'd done something like this.

The closeness between the two men was palpable. Not knowing why, India envied it, wishing to be a part somehow. She wondered if participating in threesomes was something they did often and it made her wonder if she was just another piece of ass for them? Did they want her only because she was the only woman on the island?

"We've done this before," Grant finally answered.

She closed her eyes against the harsh truth. "How many times?"

Rafe raked his fingers through his hair. "It isn't what you think."

"It doesn't matter what I think. I want to know how many times it happened."

Rafe took a seat next to her and she tensed, hoping he wouldn't touch her because if he did, she knew she'd fall into his arms.

"Several times. I can't remember how many exactly, but it was with the same woman. Before you condemn either one of us, will you at least hear us out? It's a complicated matter."

India snorted. "How complicated can it be? You two get your rocks off by tag-teaming the same woman." The second the words left her mouth, she regretted them. When put like that it sounded so dirty. Judging from the anger blazing in Rafe's amber eyes and the open-mouthed bewilderment on Grant's face, she'd gone too far.

"I'm sorry. I shouldn't have said that, but I don't understand."

Grant took her hand and brought it to his lips. "Then let us make you understand."

"Fine. Make me understand, though I doubt you could. You have to admit there's something strange about two men...well I mean men are usually so proprietary. I don't get how you two have come to the decision to do something like this."

Grant closed his eyes briefly and took a deep breath. "Like Rafe said, it's a complicated situation and you're right, the lifestyle the two of us chose is unusual, but it stems from years of friendship and similar trials we've faced. To be honest, we've only discovered we like sharing the same woman within the last couple years."

India tried to listen with an open mind, but she couldn't help interrupting. "What happened to precipitate it? Was it one drunken night at some party?"

"You're partially right," Rafe answered. "Alcohol was involved but it's not responsible for what we did. You see, the woman we shared was my wife."

India gasped. This made things weirder still. "Your wife? Are you kidding me? Was it her idea or yours? Is that the reason she divorced you? Because she could no longer handle the circumstances?"

"No. She liked what we did just fine. I was the one to file the petition for divorce. In fact, Grant and I booked this vacation to celebrate it becoming official. Angie and I had been married for a couple years and it was rocky at best. In hindsight, I never should have married her, but I was stupid and the sex was good. Anyway, Angie wasn't happy about my friendship with Grant. You see, she dated him before we were married and I think it annoyed her that I would still be friends with him. She claimed we spent too much time together. It was a bone of contention between us from the beginning even though we had other problems. That, however, seemed to be an issue that neither of us were willing to back down on. She wanted Grant out of my life and I wasn't going to tell my best friend of over twenty years to go away. It might sound cruel to you that I would choose my best friend over my wife, but it wasn't like that. I was willing to put her first in my life, even going as far as to only see Grant at work and the occasional outing to a sporting event, but Angie begrudged even that little bit of time."

From the short time she'd been with them, India could tell Grant and Rafe's bond was deeper than anything she'd ever witnessed between two non-related men. She could understand why it would have been difficult for Rafe to sever all ties with someone he'd been friends with for so long. "It sounds like she didn't want to be reasonable."

Rafe grimaced. "Not a bit. And because I wasn't willing to toe the line, the arguments grew worse. I think the last time I indulged in an argument with her, she slapped me. Believe me, I think I was very close to strangling her in that moment. My Latin temper got the better of me, and I remember shaking her, I was so enraged. I think if the phone hadn't rung, I may have ended up hurting her. I stormed out of the house and from that point on I stayed away, in some cases days at a time. I was never unfaithful to her, but the last thing I wanted was to come home to bickering after a hard day's work. One night Grant and I got smashed. He was in better shape than I was, so he drove me home. Angie was waiting. She'd been drinking as well and there were angry accusations, one of them about our sexuality."

India raised a brow in question. It was obvious they liked women, but it didn't mean they couldn't be bi. "You two aren't—"

A faint smile touched Rafe's lips. "We're many things, but not that. Both of us are one hundred percent hetero. Getting back to the story, when Angie accused Grant and I of being lovers, it was the straw that broke the camel's back. To say I was furious is an understatement, so I pushed her against the wall and started kissing and ripping her clothes off. Grant was there and before any of us could make heads or tails of what was happening, the two of us were fucking her bowlegged. I don't know if it was the alcohol, or something that would have eventually happened with the three us anyway, but it did. And from then on, there was no going back."

"Why did it end? I mean why the divorce if you were satisfied sexually?"

The corners of Rafe's mouth twitched into a humorless smile. "Marriage is more than just sex. Outside of the bedroom there was no communication. Besides that, my ex was a manipulator. Even from the beginning of the relationship she tried to pit Grant and me against each other. The new, exciting sex life only held us together for a little while. The deal breaker was discovering she'd been with other men, but I think divorce was inevitable without the cheating. Hell, if I'm being honest, all there ever was between us was the sex."

"And you two decided that you liked what you did?" she

wondered aloud.

"It was much more than that," Grant spoke up. "Angie did her best to undermine our friendship and nearly succeeded. Rafe and I have been through too much, suffered too greatly to allow that to happen again. It was more than just sex for us. Sharing a woman brought us closer together and strengthened our relationship after it had been rocked from its foundation. We're both hot-blooded men who love sex, but we're also past the age of sleeping around. We want to settle down with someone who will not only accept the friendship Rafe and I share, but be our woman, share in our lives as our partner, and live with us in a committed relationship."

"But...what about marriage and children?" she demanded, still not believing her ears. Their story rang true, but she still had trouble wrapping her head around it.

"I would like children, and Grant would too. Any children that would come out of the relationship would have two fathers and we'd raise each of them as our own, regardless of DNA. It simply wouldn't matter. We'd be a family in every sense of the word. It might not be a traditional arrangement, but we've given this a lot of thought. We want you to be that woman, and I think you knew from the start there was something between us."

India was speechless. What could she say to that? She'd just allowed both of them to make love to her, no, she'd begged them for it, so what was the point of saying she didn't want them too? But a relationship?

"Say something, India." Grant searched her face with anxious blue eyes.

"I don't know what to say. It's a lot to take in. This lifestyle you speak of is alternative to say the least, but I don't know if it's right for me."

Rafe threw a stick into the dying fire. "Are you saying that because it's what you've been programmed to think? Tell me, how did it feel when you had Grant's dick in your pussy and mine in your mouth?" Amber eyes flashed.

India looked away from his steady gaze. "Don't make me say it."

"It has to be said. You may be able to brush aside what happened, but I sure as hell won't."

"And neither will I." Grant placed a hand on her knee. "Tonight proved we're compatible sexually, but it was much more than that. Since we've been on the island, I've learned a lot about you and what I've found out I like. You're smart, sweet, compassionate, and I'm already on my way to falling in love with you."

Grant's confession made her jaw drop. She hadn't expected to hear that. India turned to Rafe. "And you? How do you feel?"

"The same. I felt a connection with you almost immediately when we met at the airport."

"I see. This gives me something to think about, but you're asking me to throw away all my ideals about what a committed relationship is and fall in line with what you two want. But how do I know for sure this would have happened if we weren't stuck on this island? Or perhaps if another female had survived, you'd be with her?"

Grant gave her hand a light squeeze. "I know it's a lot to mull over, but believe me when I say that what we feel for you is real regardless of the setting."

"But what if we never get off this place?"

Grant's mouth thinned to a tight line before he answered. "It may be something we'll have to face in the coming weeks if we're still here, but until then, we have each other."

"I did enjoy what we did," she admitted. "But I...I feel so guilty about it. Good girls don't do things like this. I've spent all my life trying to be the person people think I should be. It's hard for me to let go completely."

Rafe reached over and brushed his knuckles against her cheek. "We can help."

India wanted more than anything to give in to them, but did she dare? So far she was unlucky in love. If there was a fallout between the three of them, she'd always come up the loser if sides were taken.

After being with two men, she discovered she wanted more of the titillating passion they shared, but giving her heart was another thing. She ran her tongue over parched lips. "I do want the both of you but...until I get my feelings sorted out it can only be physical."

"We want more than just your body, India," Grant countered softly.

She nodded. "I know but it's all I have to give right now. I think I've done a pretty lousy job in the relationship department so far and I'm just not ready to have my heart engaged in something I'm not sure will sustain beyond this island."

Rafe looked as though he wanted to protest, but then shut his mouth. Finally he nodded in agreement.

India turned to Grant, silently questioning him.

"It's not what either one of us wants and what we feel for you is something much bigger than our circumstances, but if this is all you have to offer right now, we'll take it," he finished with an exasperated sigh.

Quiet swept over the cave once again only to be interrupted by the growl of her stomach. India wrapped her arms around her midsection. "I know we agreed to be careful with our rations, but I'm starving. How much coconut do we have left?"

Grant stroked his lightly bearded face. "Just one more coconut. We could share it, but in the morning we're going to have to find other things to eat. It doesn't seem like these coconut trees are dropping any more of their fruit."

"I've been trying to catch fish, but with no luck. I'll try again tomorrow, but we may also need to scour the island for animals. It might be our only hope." The grim look on Rafe's face scared the hell out of India.

Did they survive the plane crash only to starve to death?

Grant woke with a hard-on like nobody's business. India's face was pressed against his chest and her arm locked around his waist. Rafe was molded against her back, snoring soundly.

Grant wanted to wake her up and sample some more of that tight pussy, but he knew India needed her rest. The sun was starting to peak into the cave. He couldn't remain where he lay, otherwise he would end up flipping her on her back and fucking her senseless.

Fighting the urge to do just that, he slowly detangled himself from her and pulled away. He'd slipped his clothes back on in the middle of the night, not because of the cold, but because having his bare dick nestled against India's cunt would have been torturous. He gave the sleeping pair one last look before getting to his feet.

From the looks of it, they would be out a little longer. Noticing the fire burning out, he threw some wood into the ashy heap, until the flames were healthy once again.

What he needed was a good wash. His face itched like hell and Grant wished he had some razors to cut off his beard. He felt like Grizzly Adams although he was far from that point yet. Grant couldn't wait to get back to civilization. He didn't let the fact that they hadn't seen a boat or plane after all the time they'd been here discourage him. He had to keep believing they'd be rescued or else they might as well all give up on living right then and there. He'd been though too much to let things end like this.

Once he made it to the waterfall and stripped, Grant waded to the water until he was waist deep. It was cold, but at least it killed his erection. Being alone gave him time to think about last night's events. India had been so responsive and ready for both of them. He couldn't remember a time when he'd felt so whole during the act of lovemaking.

In India, he and Rafe had found the void Angie couldn't fill. Now it was only a matter of convincing India that what the three of them shared was more than just sex. From the things she'd let slip in conversation, he gathered her past was painful. Perhaps she hadn't suffered the physical and mental abuse he and Rafe had, but every now and then, he'd catch a glimpse of sadness in those doe brown eyes, making him want to take her in his arms. There was still so much he wanted to learn about her and he had every intention of doing so.

Grant splashed water over his body and wet his hair, staying in the icy pool until he couldn't stand it any longer. When he stepped out of the water, he noticed a familiar looking plant. The closer he drew to it, his certainty increased.

Aloe.

Not only would it help with the mosquito bites and patches of sunburn, if worse came to worse, the gel inside was edible. A smile tugged the corners of his lips. It would also make a very nice lubricant.

He made a mental note to pick some before he went back to

camp. The very idea of sliding his dick between her cheeks, past her tight anal ring, made his cock hard.

Grant found himself in the same predicament he'd woken up in. He palmed his cock, trying to get his body under control once again. Circling his shaft with his fingers, he pumped it in frantic motions. No woman had ever driven him to such a blistering need. It would be sheer agony until he had her again.

Closing his eyes, he attempted to soothe the beast within.

A soft gasp brought his eyes back open. Standing on the edge of the water was India, and her eyes flashed with naked, unashamed lust.

Chapter Ten

India had woken up feeling bereft, as if something was missing. That something had turned out to be someone. Grant. Over the past few days she'd grown accustomed to sleeping in between Rafe and Grant and she missed his warmth. Unable to get back to sleep, she got up and decided to head to the waterfall to wash. She figured Grant was out searching for food.

She didn't think she'd stumble upon him standing at the edge of the water, stroking his cock. He was a magnificent specimen. Grant wasn't as hairy as Rafe, but he was a bit more cut, from his sculpted pectorals to his washboard stomach down to his narrow waist and hips. And dear Lord, his cock was huge. She didn't have much of a chance to get a good look at it the night before, but in the light of day she found herself salivating.

Grant looked at her like a deer caught in the headlights. He dropped his hand and moved to grab his pants.

"Don't." She walked over to him. "I don't want you to stop."

His Adam's apple bobbed up and down his tanned throat. "Did you like seeing me touch myself?"

India never thought she'd find something like that arousing, but oddly, she did. "Yes, I do." She allowed her gaze to roam over his body.

His lips shaped into a smile. "Far be it beyond me to displease a lady." He fisted his cock again, and stroked it, his blue gaze locking with hers.

Her nipples pressed against the khaki material of Rafe's shirt. Heat rushed through the pores of her body. She wanted him. Taking a slow, deliberate step toward him, India couldn't think of anything more than running her hands all over his body. She halted when she stood mere inches from Grant.

"I want to do that." She touched the hand wrapped around his dick.

His light eyes went cobalt. "You're going to be the death of me."

India brushed his hand aside and ran her fingertips along the length of him. "But what a way to go, right?"

"Oh yeah." He chuckled. "What brought on this change? Last night you were the shy kitten, but this morning you're a seductive vixen."

She shrugged. "Maybe I've finally come to my senses." It had taken her a while to fall asleep last night and India had a lot of time to think. She'd liked what they did together way too much to deny them or herself anymore. India wanted to live and feel and heaven knows she'd never felt the way she did when she was with Rafe and Grant.

Lowering herself before him until she rested on her knees, she grasped his hard rod. "My, you're big."

"All the better to fuck you with, my dear."

She giggled. "You're nasty. I thought Rafe was the bad one."

"I have my moments and there's definitely something about seeing a beautiful woman kneeling before me, ready to suck my dick that brings out the perv in me."

India smiled before circling the helmet-shaped tip with her

tongue.

The heat emanating from his cock nearly scorched her taste buds as she stroked him with her lips.

"That's it, sweetheart, lick it." He grabbed tufts of her hair in either fist.

Tightening her fingers around his cock, she opened wide and took him into her mouth. Slowly she sucked him deep and hard, trying to take as much of his dick in as she could. Savoring his musky masculine flavor, India found herself highly turned on by her act of fellatio. She slid her free hand inside her panties and fingered her clit.

"Oh, India. That feels so good."

She gripped her lips around his member, sliding them up and down with a bob of her head. His fingers clenched her hair harder, but she didn't notice or feel pain. She was much too aroused to care.

Though she really enjoyed what happened with the three of them the night before, India liked the one on one time with Grant. Maybe she would get the chance to be alone with Rafe as well, but that would come later. In the meantime, she planned on getting acquainted with Grant's awesome physique.

As her head jerked back and forth and she frantically sucked his cock, India released her clit and slipped two fingers inside her damp pussy.

"India, if you don't stop now, I'm going to come in your mouth."

She parted her lips and released his cock to look up at him. "Would that be a bad thing?"

"Hell no. I would love it."

"Then shut up and let me do my thing." She took him back into her mouth, sliding her lips along him, faster and with more intensity. India worked her fingers in and out of her box, so turned on she was close to her own orgasm. Working his dick with ferocious strokes of her mouth, milking him, she fingered her pussy in rhythm.

Suddenly, Grant let out a primal shout. "India!" He thrust his hips forward, the tip of his cock touching the back of her throat, before he filled her mouth with a warm flood of his salty seed.

India gulped his come, slurping each drop. The sensual act of swallowing his come pushed her to a powerful peak that racked through her body. It took every ounce of control she possessed to keep her lips wrapped around his cock. Only when she was sure she had every bit of his essence did she finally pull her fingers from her wet channel, let go of his dick and get to her feet. Grant was still shaking with his desire.

He wrapped his arms around her waist and kissed India gently on the lips. "Sweetheart, you didn't have to do that."

"I know I didn't, but I wanted to." She was content to be held within the circle of his steely arms. A thought occurred to her and she lifted her head to meet his gaze. "Do you think Rafe would mind about what just happened? I'm not really sure how this thing is supposed to work between us."

Grant kissed her forehead and gave her an easy smile, showing off his deep dimples. "He won't mind as I'm sure there will be times when the two of you will be together when I'm not around. But of course, most of the time the three of us will be together. Will you be okay with that?"

She nodded. "Yes. I've already resigned myself to it." India placed her head against his chest, listening to his heartbeat, not wanting to leave his embrace. "Why didn't the two of you come inside of me last night? I'm on the shot so you needn't worry about me getting pregnant."

Grant's chest rose and fell from the deep breath and exhale. "We wanted to, you have no idea how much, but it was our way of showing you some consideration. The decision for us to do that would have to come from you. It would seal our pact. Last night was our first time together and you were apprehensive and uncertain."

"But I'm not anymore."

Grant nuzzled the side of her neck. "That much is obvious."

"I've never had sex without a condom before. Is it totally irresponsible of me to want the two of you to finish inside of me?"

"No. If that's what you feel, you can't be condemned for that, but if it makes you feel any better, I get tested regularly for STD's and my results are always negative. Rafe can attest to his clean bill of health. Does that ease your mind?"

For some odd reason, India was never really worried about that. Sure it would normally have been a concern for her, but with Rafe and Grant the same rules didn't apply. It was strange feeling this way about two men she'd know for the space of a week, especially when in today's society having sex unprotected was like playing Russian Roulette with one's health. Not knowing why, something told her these men would never endanger her in any way. The thought was scary and comforting at the same time.

Grant placed another kiss at the side of her neck. "Okay, sweetheart. Why don't you go wash up and I'll be on the beach trying to scrounge up something to eat. I'm sure Rafe is probably stirring now."

India nodded, reluctant to let him go. She pouted as she watched him dress.

He walked over to some plants and began picking the long fat leaves. He then turned to wink at her before leaving.

There was something mischievous in the look he'd shot her, and she wondered what he was up to. Whatever it was, she had a feeling she was in for a sleepless night.

ε၁

The stick Rafe had fashioned into a spear broke in half at his last failed attempt in catching a fish. "Shit!" This was frustrating as hell. He'd been standing in the water for God knows how long trying to catch a fish and he couldn't get one even though he could clearly see them swimming beneath the surface.

He had to catch something or tonight they'd go hungry. He saw Grant a few feet away, using his shirt as a makeshift net. It didn't seem like he was having much luck either. They had to get off this damn island soon. In the week they'd been here, he could already tell he'd lost some weight. Right now, he'd give his left nut for a cheeseburger with all the fixings.

The sun beat against his back and Rafe wished he had the protection of his shirt. He'd have a nasty burn by the end of the day if he stood out here much longer.

India, who had been gathering firewood earlier, joined him. His heart skipped a beat when he saw her. "No luck, huh?"

He shook his head. "Not a bit. It's not as easy as they make it look on television, and I've broken my stick."

"Nothing ever is that easy. I know this isn't an ideal situation, but on that big rock over there, I saw a bunch of snails. If we cook them over a fire they won't taste so bad."

Rafe turned his nose up. He was hungry, but not that damn hungry. "I'm sorry, but I'm not eating snails."

"Haven't you ever had escargot? It's pretty tasty in a garlic butter sauce."

Rafe wanted to throw up. It was bad enough he'd eaten that raw crab on their second night here. It had done a number on his stomach and there was no telling what those slimy mollusks would do to him. "No thanks. I believe I'll pass on that."

"I'll pick some just in case. I'm sure they probably won't taste like they do in the restaurant, but we may not have a choice."

She was right. Beggars couldn't be choosers. "You sound as if you've had them often."

"I have. They're not bad, actually—a little chewy, but still quite tasty."

"Ugh. Please don't go into detail."

India laughed, a pleasant tinkling sound. "Sorry. I guess we all have different tastes. Actually my favorite food is hot dogs in any form, chili-cheese dogs, hot off the grill and corndogs. I even like them raw."

"Raw?"

"They taste just like bologna. I bet I could beat the reigning hot dog eating champion's record when it comes to wolfing down those bad boys."

Rafe smiled. "A woman after my own heart. You don't strike me as the hot dog type. I could imagine a classy lady like you eating Lobster Thermador and Filet Mignon."

India shrugged. "I like those things too, but I think my palate prefers more simple fare. Growing up, hot dogs and hamburgers were a treat. The only time I could get them were at cook outs or when I was staying with other relatives for a visit. My mother took a cordon bleu class and we would have exotic dishes every night. My parents are food snobs. While other kids got mac and cheese or chicken nuggets, I got duck à l'orange."

"Sounds like you had a good life."

A shadow crossed her face and again, that sadness he'd noticed before entered her eyes. "I don't think so. I would have preferred the mac and cheese. Maybe it's the grass is greener syndrome."

Rafe felt a sudden burst of anger. India didn't have the right to resent her upbringing, especially, from the sounds of it, since she had it so good compared to him. She sounded downright ungrateful. Considering there were days his mother didn't remember his existence, he could only have hoped to have a gourmet meal fixed for him every night. "The grass isn't always greener, India. At least you had two parents who cared about you, fed and clothed you. You had the life didn't you?" Rafe couldn't keep the bitterness from his tone as he thought of his own harrowing childhood.

India's eyes widened and she back away from him with a gasp as if he'd struck her. "Is that what you think? Having two parents doesn't guarantee a happy childhood."

He raised a brow in challenge. "Lady, I think I have you beat hands down as far as shitty upbringings go."

Her mouth thinned to an angry line, her eyes narrowing. "I don't know enough about your life to judge how bad it's been, nor do you know about mine. I might have had privileges a lot of children didn't, but everything I've ever been given by my parents was done grudgingly. Did you have to grow up in the shadow of an older sibling knowing they could never do any wrong and you could do no right? Do you know what it's like to know your folks loved that sibling so much more than they could ever love you?"

"Are you sure it wasn't all in your mind?"

India glared at him. "It's not very hard to imagine when you're told you were a mistake. Or how about being told you've ruined their lives by being born, what an embarrassment you are, how you'll never be any good, how unattractive and stupid you are. Whenever I had a friend and worked up the nerve to bring them home, my parents found something wrong with them. My grades were never good enough. If I brought home a B, it should have been an A. If I brought home an A it should have been an A plus. If I brought home an A plus it had to have been a fluke. Everything good in my life or anything I enjoyed they crushed. Oh, on the surface they were the perfect parents, smiling in the faces of people who didn't know them like I did, but I knew the truth." Her eyes glistened.

Rafe moved toward her, but she shook her head, and put her arm out to give them distance.

"I didn't know..."

"Yet you decided to pass judgment on me anyway? Since you seem so curious about my life you might as well hear the rest."

"India, please—"

She continued as though she hadn't been interrupted. "Do you know, they didn't bother coming to even one of my school events? I was valedictorian of my class, but they decided to take a vacation the same week of my graduation. They didn't come to my high school, college or law school graduation. My brother Jack never made the honor roll. He scraped by with Cs, he was disrespectful and talked back to my parents, but they treated him like a king. He got a car for his sixteenth birthday. I got a card with a five dollar gift certificate to a five and dime store, which by the way my mother got in the mail. My brother got all the praise and didn't appreciate it a bit, while I got pushed in the background. All I ever wanted was for them to say to me that they were proud of me, or that I did a good job on something. The only thing I received from them in abundance was criticism." By now the tears were streaming down her face.

Rafe felt like a jerk. He moved to take her in his arms, but she backed away again.

"Don't touch me! You wanted to hear it, fine, you're going to get all the dirty details. As I was saying, nothing was ever good enough for them, until the day I finally met a man who won their approval. He was rich, good looking and from a wealthy, politically-connected family. I was so brainwashed into believing my goal in life was to please them, I ended up engaged to the guy. I even convinced myself I loved him, because it was the only way I could justify being with someone who didn't really value me as a person. Do you know what my mom said to me shortly after we announced our engagement?"

"What?" Rafe could tell by the pain in her eyes it was difficult for her to relive these memories.

"She said, 'I'm glad you finally did something that didn't make me regret not aborting you'."

Rafe's mouth dropped opened. He thought *his* mother was a piece of work, but it seemed that India's was just as monstrous. "She didn't, did she?"

India nodded. "It's not the worst thing she's ever said, or my father for that matter. Besides, I was so starved for their approval that comment actually made me happy. Can you imagine how warped a person has to be to live off of crumbs like that?"

"So what happened between you and your fiancé?"

"I stayed engaged to Steven even though he treated me like his dumb trophy arm piece. He never listened when I had an opinion and when I did dare to voice one, he was condescending and told me to just be quiet and look pretty. Considering I let go of a great guy just because my parents didn't think he came from the right background, Steven was all I believed I deserved.

I tried to hang on, but finding him in bed with another woman made me realize I couldn't be with him no matter how much I tried to fool myself that I could. I broke off the relationship in public at the engagement party. My parents were furious. They didn't even care about what he'd done. They were angry because they had lost their chance of being connected to such a powerful family. My feelings weren't taken into consideration. So you see. The grass may not be greener, but it certainly can't be any browner."

She wiped the wet trails from her cheeks before turning on her heel, leaving Rafe where he stood, wishing he'd kept his big mouth shut.

Chapter Eleven

The snails weren't so bad once they'd been cooked in the fire. They tasted nothing like the escargot in the restaurants, but it was a welcome change from the coconuts. Grant and Rafe hadn't managed to catch fish, but they'd caught a few more crabs.

This time, with the fire, the food was much more palatable. For the first time in several days, India's stomach was content. She pulled the stick away from the fire and studied the charred mollusk she'd speared with it. When she was satisfied it was cooked all the way through, she picked it off the tip and popped it in her mouth.

The men had been reluctant to try them, but they eventually broke down and gave them a shot, preferring that over hunger. It must not have been so awful for them, because they ate several more.

No one said much around the fire as they ate, but India felt it was time for them to have a little talk concerning her earlier outburst. After telling Rafe a few home truths, he had tried to approach her, but she wasn't having it. Now that she'd had some time to cool down, India was able to think about the situation more clearly.

From snippets of their prior conversations, she was able to discern that Rafe and Grant may have experienced some childhood trauma. When put in that context, she could understand where Rafe's anger may have come from. He probably believed she was being an ungrateful brat. Now she had to know what happened to them in their past. Maybe it would give her some kind of clue as to the closeness between the two men.

"Rafe," she cleared her throat. "I hope there aren't any hard feelings about today."

Rafe shot her a smile and she knew all was forgiven. He put down the stick he'd been holding over the fire, before moving across the cave to sit next to her. He placed his hand on her knee. "I'm sorry about what I said. I had no right to make those assumptions. I was unreasonably angry. This temper of mine gets the best of me sometimes."

India placed her hand against his bearded cheek. "It's alright. I think I understand why you were upset and I know this is asking a lot, but would you tell me about it?"

Rafe withdrew his hand and clenched his fist at his side. "It's not something I like talking about."

She continued to stroke the side of his face. "Do you think it was easy for me to share stories about my dysfunctional family? I can assure you it wasn't, but now that it's out in the open, I'm glad the two of you know." India knew Rafe had told Grant what she'd said because of the understanding looks he'd shot her through the day. She appreciated his lack of pity which made her certain he knew how she felt.

Rafe finally nodded. "I guess it's only fair, but I'm warning you, it's not a pretty story."

"They never are." India dropped her hand and placed it in her lap, waiting for him to begin.

He gulped hard, opened his mouth, then closed it again, obviously not able to get the words out.

"Maybe I should start," Grant broke in from the other side of her.

Rafe's gratitude was evident as he bowed his head.

Grant seemed as if he too was having trouble finding the right words to say, but finally he began. "Rafe and I met when we were kids. He and his mom moved next door to my father and me. I saw him around school but we never really hung out until the night Rafe was thrown out of his house in the freezing cold by his mother's latest boyfriend. I offered him a place to sleep that night and we've been friends ever since."

India knew she was getting the very short version of the story and realized she'd have to ask questions if she wanted to learn more.

"Why would your mother's boyfriend kick you out, Rafe? How old were you?"

Rafe kept his head lowered, his body shaking. He licked his lips before answering. "Because I wouldn't let that motherfucker touch me again."

What he said wasn't spoken much more than a whisper, but she got the message loud and clear.

India's hand flew to her mouth in shock. "You don't mean...he didn't try to..."

"Tried and succeeded on several occasions, only that night I fought back. My mother was passed out drunk as usual and Julio had come for one of his nightly visits. You see, the house was his and my mom and I were there on his sufferance or so he liked to tell me. He said I'd have to earn my keep. Whenever I cried, he'd beat me, pummeling me with his fists until I was too battered and weak to protest. I was only ten years old, goddammit!" Pain, anger and shame radiated from his every pore.

"Oh, my God." India whispered her astonishment.

118

Rafe continued. "My pleas for mercy never affected him, and he did things to me that made me ashamed to be alive. I wanted to die and had tried to kill myself, but for some twist of fast, the pills on my mom's dresser only made me mildly drowsy, and I didn't know I had to slit my wrist horizontally to do any real damage. I can't even remember my other failed attempts."

India's heart bled for him as the anger welled within her. How could anyone do something so horrific to a child? "Did you talk to your mom about it?"

Rafe let out a self-deprecating laugh. "Julio wasn't the first of my mother's boyfriends who used his fists to communicate—he was only the most perverted." He spat on the ground, underlining his disgust. "Of course that bitch who called herself my mother knew what was going on and welcomed it. She didn't give too shits about anything beyond where her next drink or drug would come from. She was going to put me in a home before she moved in with Julio, but he insisted I come with her. Oh, she knew all right. When I would cry, she'd tell me to shut up and not mess up her good thing."

India wasn't sure if she could listen to anymore. Hearing his story hurt her. She was physically ill for what Rafe had gone through, but her curiosity got the better of her. "What happened that night?"

Amber eyes glistened with the suspicious sheen of tears and India wanted to wrap her arms around him. "He came to my room and told me to put my mouth on his dick. I cried and begged him to leave me alone, but he choked me until I nearly passed out. I don't know what happened, but something inside of me snapped. When he grabbed my head to bring it to his crotch, I latched on and bit him. Hard. I clamped down like a pit bull, not letting go until he bled. I think I would have severed it if he hadn't punched me on the side of my head. The blow was enough to send me reeling. I let go, but not before I got in a few kicks. He told me to sleep outside for the night. I had nowhere to go, so I sat on the porch."

"That's when I came outside. Our row homes were connected and I heard the screams. I saw him out of my window sitting there," Grant continued. "My father was out on another one of his binge drinking excursions. I don't think he even came home that week if I recall correctly, but Rafe ended up staying with me for a couple days. We learned what we unfortunately most had in common was being used as human punching bags. My dad only got violent after he drank. Too bad that happened to be all the time. The funny thing is, I don't think he did it because he hated me. He was just a miserable son of a bitch." Grant snorted in derision.

India didn't realize she would open this can of worms when she pressured them to confide in her. "I'm so sorry."

Grant's lip twitched. "Not half as sorry as I was. It's a shame we can't pick our families. My dad was just an angry man, a loser in life: the type who always blames everyone for problems they brought on themselves. He blamed his boss for not giving him a promotion, despite never showing up for work on time. That earned me my first cracked rib. Then he was passed over again, for a minority, and he was mad at, as he put it, those goddamn liberals for implementing affirmative action. Keep in mind, my father probably wasn't a model employee, but you couldn't tell him that. Let me see, what did I get for that one? Oh yeah, two black eyes and a concussion. Then there was the time he got fired for showing up drunk at work. I got a broken nose for that offense. Then—"

"Stop!" India covered her ears with the palms of her hands, before bursting into loud sobs. What they must have been through. Neglectful as her parents had been, they never laid a hand on her, although she wasn't sure if physical abuse would have been worse than the mental cruelty. "I can't listen to anymore. I know I asked, but...I..."

Grant tugged her hands away from her ears. "Don't cry, sweetheart."

She couldn't stop. Her tears were for what all three of them had suffered. They may have survived, but they all still bore the scars. "But...but what you two had to deal with. It hurts me to know what happened to you."

"But you suffered too, India. You didn't deserve the treatment you received from your parents either. But something good came out of this."

She met crystal blue eyes. "What good could possibly come out of this mess?"

"I found Rafe and we helped each other through. Rafe's mother stayed with Julio for a few more years and my father got worse, but we made it. I think I would have died inside if not for him. That's why our bond is so strong. It's important no one come between us again the way Angie did, but we do want to settle down with someone special. Understanding the inevitability of wanting a stable relationship with a woman is why the lifestyle we've chosen is so important to us." Grant rested his arm around her shoulders and India leaned into his warmth.

She finally understood. It made sense why their friendship was so deep. It also explained the affinity she felt toward these two. They'd known the deep pain of a traumatic childhood as well. But at least they had each other. Now more than anything she wanted to be a part of it. She wanted to be their woman, heart, body and soul.

India held her hand out to Rafe, who took it and slid over to them. He brushed his lips against the side of her neck. "Need you," he growled. He nuzzled her with his hair-roughened face, his whiskers tickling her skin.

She wanted to be with them right now and wash away the pain. She turned her head to meet Rafe's lips. His kiss was desperate and hungry, like a man trying to drive away his demons. India wanted to give them the comfort of her body and in turn ease some of her past hurts as well.

Grant rubbed her thighs, sliding his hand along her skin until it reached her panties.

India parted her legs, granting him access. She loved having his fingers on her pussy and playing with her clit, fucking her. While Grant explored her pussy, she swirled her tongue around Rafe's, matching his need with her own burning ache. She sampled the hot cavern of his mouth, reveling in his wild, untamed passion for her.

Eager to feel his naked flesh pressed against hers, she worked on his pants. Rafe broke the kiss to help her, frantically clawing his way out of his clothing with hurried movements.

India anchored her body on the heels of her hands, and lifted her hips enough for Grant to slide her damp panties down her legs. She sighed as his fingertips crested along her wet slit. "Don't tease me," she pleaded.

Grant leaned over to nibble her earlobe as he slipped two fingers past her labia and pinched her clit. "Do you like that?"

India groaned. "You know I do."

Grant increased the pressure, clamping tightly onto her hot button until she gasped with pleasure-pain. "How about this?"

"I think you're trying to kill me." India said the words breathlessly.

"Only with pleasure, sweetheart." He bit down on the meaty part of her ear.

India squirmed, her pussy pulsing as Grant continued to

tease her until she was nearly insane with desire.

Rafe, naked, moved to the other side of her and gently pushed India on her back, forcing Grant to let go of her ear. "Raise your arms, baby."

Without giving it a thought, she did as she was told, knowing that ecstasy was on its way. Rafe yanked the shirt over her head, baring her body to his hungry amber gaze.

She could tell he wanted her badly by the way his hands shook. The naked passion in his eyes sent a shiver down India's spine, but still, he only stared at her, unmoving.

"Touch me, Rafe." India reached over to run her palm down his golden chest, but he caught her wrists in one hand and held them over her head.

"Just let me look at you."

She giggled nervously. "You're making me self-conscious."

Rafe placed a gentle kiss against her cheek. "You have no reason to be. You're gorgeous and don't you ever forget it."

India would have answered, but Grant shoved yet another finger into her pussy. "Sweet Jesus," she moaned.

Grant bent over and placed a kiss on her stomach before circling her navel with his tongue. She wiggled beneath his questing lips as he slowly moved his fingers in and out of her. India couldn't get enough when he did this to her.

Rafe, not to be ignored, dipped his head, opening wide over one hard-tipped breast, sucking as much of it in his mouth as he could.

The added stimulation had her jerking uncontrollably. "Yes, that's it! Don't stop. Please don't ever stop."

Grant twisted his fingers inside of her, stretching her vaginal walls further than she thought they'd go, but somehow he managed. It hurt so good she could barely think properly.

Rafe lifted his head and then transferred his attention to her other breast, nipping and licking it with savage abandon. He cupped and kneaded them in his palms and pushed them together. "You have such responsive nipples." He emphasized with a stroke of his tongue. "I can play with these beauties all day."

India wished she could answer, but she was too caught up in what both men were doing to her body. She moved with them, as they took her to the heights of desire and back. She could hardly stand it.

Biting her bottom lip, she tossed her head from side to side. Grant inched his finger out of her slick channel and slid his middle finger along the crack of her ass. Instinctively, she clenched her cheeks together.

"Relax, sweetheart. I only want to make you feel good."

She met his blue gaze with a shake of her head. "But not without lube."

"Do you trust me, India?"

Slowly, she nodded.

"Then trust that I won't do anything to hurt you. If ever there's a time when I do something that you don't like, you can tell me and I'll stop."

And she believed him. India willed her muscles to loosen, preparing herself for what would come next."

Grant circled her anus with the tip of his finger before pushing it inside her rectum. India wiggled her bottom as he fingered her panic button.

He slid his finger into her knuckle deep then eased it out to the fingernail, before sliding it back into her ass. Something like this shouldn't have felt so good, but it did.

Dear sweet Jesus, it did.

Rafe ran a trail of wet kisses on her fevered skin. He moved his hand down the length of her body until it was where Grant's hand had been. He squeezed the swollen lips of her sex together, making her moan. She bucked her hips against his erotic assault, wanting his fingers inside of her.

"You're ready for me aren't you?" Rafe grinned at her.

She moistened her suddenly dry lips. "Do you even have to ask?"

"I have something better than my fingers, baby. I think it's time my cock became reacquainted with your pussy."

India laughed, warmed by the intimate camaraderie. "I think my pussy would like that very much, so how about less talking and more action." She poked her tongue out at him.

Rafe looked at Grant. "Did you hear the lady, my friend? I think we'd better give her what she wants."

Grant winked at her. "I couldn't agree more."

India sighed when he slowly removed his finger from her rear. Grant stood up and undressed, then moved to another part of the cave to retrieve something that appeared to be long and green. That was what she'd seen him pick earlier.

She frowned, wondering what he planned on doing with it. Grant walked back over where she and Rafe lay, his hard cock bobbing with each step he took. Gulping, she couldn't tear her gaze away from his magnificence.

When he knelt next to her, he showed her what he was holding. "Do you know what this is?"

She shook her head.

"It's aloe."

India moistened her lips. "Like in the lotion?"

"Yes, but there are many more uses for it." Grant peeled the leaf apart to reveal a clear gel inside. India didn't have to be a rocket scientist to figure out what he intended to do with it. A tremble rolled up her body.

His smile widened. "So you do know what I'm going to do with it, don't you?"

"Yes," she croaked, not trusting herself to say more.

Rafe slid his body along hers and positioned India on her side. Her breathing came out short and ragged as Grant moved behind her and parted her cheeks. He slathered a dollop of the cool gel against the puckered bud of her anus.

Rafe held her steady as Grant pushed his fingers into her ass, getting her nice and slick. India rested her forehead against Rafe's chest with a sigh. She was almost too scared to move. By the time Grant replaced his fingers with the head of his cock against her ass, India was shaking in anticipation.

She dug her nails into the tops of Rafe's shoulders. "Now. Do it now!"

Grant pushed into her with one powerful thrust.

"Oh!" she cried out at the forceful invasion.

Grant placed a kiss on the back of her neck. "Did I hurt you?" he asked with apparent concern.

"It's really tight, but it doesn't hurt." India waited with baited breath until he moved again, sliding his cock deeper into her until his pelvis rested against the seat of her ass. "Grant," she sighed with utter contentment. The only thing that would make this moment perfect was to have Rafe inside of her pussy.

As if he'd read her mind, Rafe grasped her thigh, and lifted it just enough for him to position his dick against the cleft of her sex.

"Don't make me wait, Rafe."

"Never, baby. I'll never make you wait." And with that, he thrust forward. "Oh, baby, yeah." A growl of contentment escaped his throat.

India could barely breathe—barely move or speak from the mind-boggling sensation flowing through every inch of her body. Never did she think she'd experience something so decadent as being filled and deliciously stretched by two big, hard cocks.

At first, the men remained still as though giving her a chance to adjust to them being inside of her. She didn't want them to be gentlemen right now. India wanted them to fuck her. Moving her hips back and forth, she silently demanded they take her with slow, deliberate strokes.

Her grip tightened on Rafe's shoulders. Being with the two of them was like a cleansing of souls. She knew she'd lived for this very moment, to be together with Rafe and Grant, here, just like this. Words couldn't quite express all the emotions flowing through her veins. All the pain, abuse and neglect no longer mattered.

They had each other, and this joining of their bodies validated why they needed each other so much. The three of them moved together. An ungovernable fire burned inside her very core, threatening to consume them all.

India knew her climax was near. "Rafe! Grant!" She tightened her muscles around their cocks, pulling them deeper into her holes with the intention of driving them to the edge of insanity as they had done to her.

"India!" the men shouted in unison.

Their bodies slammed and mashed against each other, pulling and pushing, rubbing and loving. Sweat beaded her skin as the heat within increased with each passing second. India didn't want this moment to end, but her peak came swift and hard, starting from the tip of her toes and ending at the top of her head. It was so powerful she nearly fainted from pleasure.

Her pussy gushed, soaking the inside of her thighs.

Rafe and Grant continued to move into her, pushing and straining. Shortly after her own climax, each man shouted their release, filling her pussy and ass with their seed, steadily pumping with huffed breaths.

India felt like a boneless heap of nerves when they finally eased out of her. Rafe rolled onto his back and pulled her against his chest while Grant molded his body against her back.

No words needed to be spoken. This just felt right.

So right.

Chapter Twelve

India frowned as she ran her fingers along her ribcage. The fact that she could actually see the outline of her bones beneath her skin was frustrating. They'd been on this island for what felt like years. They had kept track of their days on the island by marking the inside of the cave and they were on day fifty-seven.

Fifty-damn-seven days and they were still here!

She'd dropped an uncomfortable amount of weight, her body was covered in bug bites and her eating habits had wreaked havoc on her digestive system. Grant and Rafe had lost weight as well—to the point they were beginning to lose muscle tone. Without razors for a proper shave, both men sported thick, bushy beards. Their clothes were tattered shreds. If they stayed here any longer they'd look like three refugees. No. That wasn't true. They already did. If they remained, they'd look like hungry zombies.

There were days when one of them managed to catch a fish or two and when they didn't, there were snails, coconuts and the occasional crabs. Once they'd resorted to eating bugs. She shuddered to think about what they had to do to exist, but it was either that or die. The almost daily rain would have depressed a circus clown, but somehow they managed.

If it weren't for Rafe and Grant being with her, she wasn't sure what she would have done. With each day that passed, she found herself falling a little more in love with each man.

What India liked most about Rafe was his forcefulness and his straight-forwardness. Grant's strength was his sweet consideration and silent strength. They both made her laugh, and made her happy despite their circumstances. They were protective of her, making India feel the love she'd desperately longed for in her life. For the first time in her twenty-eight years, she was content.

Wait. She was twenty-nine now. Her birthday would have been a couple weeks ago by her estimation, but she hadn't brought it up to either of the men. Just lasting another day on the island was gift enough.

They spent most of their days scrounging the island for food, wood and any needed supplies. Sometimes they'd frolic in the ocean, or laze in the sand until the sun was at its peak. Then they would either find shade or retreat to the cave. She'd learned more about each of them and in turn, shared details of her life.

Their nights were filled with earth-shattering sex that rocked her body to its core. She looked forward to those moments.

With a yawn she looked out over the horizon. India felt lethargic today and didn't have much energy to do anything other than sit on the edge of the water, letting the waves run over her legs. Rafe was in the cave, trying to restart the fire that had gone out this morning. Grant was off on a hunt, determined to catch an animal. They had discovered some larger animals deeper in the woods, but they had yet to be successful at catching anything of significance. She still wished Grant luck on his *Lord of the Flies*-like quest.

India wiggled her toes in the water, simply letting her mind wander. At first the faint buzzing sound in the distance didn't register, until it drew closer. Glancing up in the sky, she blinked once, then twice, not believing her eyes.

After all this time...a plane!

Scrambling to her feet, she ran along the beach, waving her hands frantically, hoping the pilot would notice the SOS sign they'd made out of leaves and coconut shells.

"Plane!" she shouted at the top of her lungs hoping it would bring the men over. "Plane!" India hurried along the beach. She continued jumping up and down. Just then, Grant appeared, frantically signaling to the plane.

She didn't know what to expect, but the vehicle kept going without circling or indicating they'd been spotted, much to her disappointment. But for the first time in several days, there was hope. "Do you think they saw us?" She turned to Grant.

"It was low enough to the ground. If they didn't see us, then hopefully they saw our distress sign."

Rafe joined them a few minutes later. "I got the fire started again. What was all the commotion?"

"Didn't you hear it? We saw a plane!" India could barely contain her excitement. She'd been feeling pretty pessimistic about getting off the island of late, so the renewal of hope was just the thing she needed.

Rafe shouted in glee, grabbing India by the waist and twirling her around until she was dizzy.

"Put me down, you big oaf." She administered a playful slap against his arm.

He put her down with a laugh. "I wish I would have been out here to see it myself, but just knowing one flew by is good enough for me."

India didn't want to be the voice of doom and gloom, but she had to be realistic. "Unfortunately, there's no guarantee they saw us. And even if they did, there's no telling whether they'll care."

Grant gave her a little pat on the rear. "You're right, but we have to think positive."

"But after being here for nearly two months, it makes me wonder if anyone would expect to find us here. I'm not trying to be a downer, but I'm worried."

"Don't be worried, honey. I'm sure they must have seen something." Grant sounded more upbeat than he had in the past several days. Even though he was the one who always tried to look on the bright side of things, lately it seemed as if he had been losing hope as well.

A scary thought crossed her mind. "We've been gone all this time. People probably think we're dead. I mean, you two have a business to go back to, but my job has probably been filled. Public defenders are a dime a dozen. Then my apartment has probably been rented out. God knows where my stuff is. If my parents had anything to do with it, they probably tossed it and I'm sure they won't appreciate me staying with them until I get another place."

Rafe's brows knitted together. "You're not going back to them. You're staying with us."

On the island it was easy to be with the two of them and to let go completely, but how would things be in the real world? They'd talked about their future together, but would it play out as they'd planned?

India merely nodded, not voicing her concerns. Scared about what would happen to them. She didn't want to think about losing either man, but could their love sustain once they settled back into their lives?

೮ youngest

"Would you like more coffee, Mr. Thompson?" This will be the last time I'll be serving drinks before the flight lands." The flight attendant gave Grant a toothy grin. She allowed her gaze to roam over his body, leaving no doubt in his mind that she wanted more than to serve him coffee. Under other circumstances, he would have flirted back, but he had too much on his mind to give her much attention.

Soon they'd be landing on U.S. soil for the first time in over two and a half months. That wouldn't be such a bad thing if it weren't for the fact that the media had somehow gotten wind of their story, of the plane crash and how the three of them had managed to survive on the island for the length of time they had.

Grant waved his hand dismissively. "No thanks. Three's my limit." He shot her a brief smile then turned away to look out the window.

She obviously didn't get the hint. "If you don't mind my being so bold, I just wanted to tell you how brave I think you are. Your story is amazing."

That's all he'd heard over the past weeks and frankly, he was getting bored with it, but she couldn't possibly know that. "Thank you. We all did what we had to do. If it weren't for my companions, I doubt I would have fared so well."

"You're being modest," she persisted, tossing an auburn lock over her shoulder. "I saw your interview on the *Anne Webster Show*. I'm sure most people wouldn't have made it a few days, let alone fifty-seven. I have to finish serving the rest of the passengers, but when I walk by again, do you think you could autograph something for me?"

Grant resisted the urge to roll his eyes, but remained calm. "Sure."

"Great. I should be done in about fifteen minutes."

He was glad to see the back of her, not comfortable with the attention. That day they had spotted the plane, Grant prayed someone inside had spotted them. His wishes were granted when the next morning a rescue boat came for them and took them to the closest inhabited island, which ironically turned out to be their original destination, Fuamatuu Island.

They were put into a hotel and given new clothes and spending money while their passport situation was sorted out. Some calls back home assured him their business had been in good hands. The crazy thing was, they had all simply been declared missing, since there had been neither sign of the plane nor any signal as to where it had landed. From what Grant understood, the story had been the plane had pulled an Amelia Earhart, simply vanishing.

Somehow, the media had gotten a hold of their story, sensationalizing it. It started with a local news station on the island, and then began to spread like wildfire, making them instant celebrities. Everyone wanted to get the first interview with them, from Larry King to Diane Sawyer. The three of them couldn't go anywhere on the island without a reporter trying to talk to them. Newsgroups from all over the world wanted a piece of them, and the attention was nerve-wracking to say the least.

They finally gave in and participated in a group interview with Anne Webster, only because she was the least annoying out of the bunch. The interview didn't go too badly, but it was something Grant didn't wish to repeat.

Another problem with being under public scrutiny was he, Rafe and India couldn't have the time alone they wanted. They had separate rooms at the hotel and only managed to get together a couple times because it seemed like their every move was being watched.

Then there was India herself. She didn't say anything, but he could feel her withdrawal. It scared the hell out of him to think she would turn her back on what they shared out of fear of what other people would say. He knew Rafe wasn't happy about the situation either.

India and Rafe sat in the seats across the aisle from his. She was asleep, with her head on Rafe's shoulder. His friend was casually thumbing through a magazine. Grant leaned over his chair. "Rafe."

"The other man turned his gaze in Grant's direction. "What?"

"What do you think will happen when we land?"

"We go home. Try to settle back into a routine and get our business affairs in order. Then we start living as we planned."

What they'd discussed on the island was selling their respective properties, with India moving to the Philadelphia area to live with them, so they could all purchase a home together. "You sound so sure it's going to happen exactly as we planned."

Rafe shrugged. "Why wouldn't it? I'm certain of my feelings. Are you having doubts?"

"About how I feel for her? No."

"Then what's the problem? I don't want to be with anyone else and neither do you. You sound a little too unsure for my comfort."

Grant sighed. "It's not that, but I'm beginning to wonder about India's feelings. She's been distant lately, and I can't help remembering that comment she made during the interview about getting back to her old life."

"I'm sure she didn't mean it the way it sounded. I've noticed her distance too, but it's probably just nerves. Don't worry. Everything will go according to plan."

"But if it doesn't?" Grant wanted to know.

A determine gleam sparked in Rafe's eyes. "It will."

"If you say so."

"I do."

"How do we handle all this attention we've been getting lately? I for one can't take much more of it."

Rafe shrugged. "We probably fell victim to a slow news week. Had we been discovered when something important was going on, I'm quite sure this wouldn't have happened. Relax, the media has a short attention span. This will probably blow over in a few days or until the next big story comes along. Right now, I'm looking forward to starting our new life together with our woman."

That certainly sounded nice, but Grant wondered if India was still of the same mind.

Chapter Thirteen

India stared out the bay window of her aunt's living room, watching children play a game of tag. She wrapped her arms around her body, wishing they belonged to Rafe or Grant. When their plane had landed in New York, the three of them only had a few minutes together before she had to catch her connecting flight. A brief hug with each of them had been all they'd shared, because she knew if she'd allowed them to kiss and hold her, she wouldn't want to leave.

She hadn't seen them in over a week but talked on the phone with them every night while they sorted out their business affairs. India missed each of them with every depth of her being. She hadn't gotten much sleep since she'd been back.

Things had been chaotic at best. Just as India knew she would be, her aunt Val was waiting to pick her up from the airport, but surprisingly so were her parents. She was so struck by the hugs and kisses, it didn't register at first that the only reason they'd shown up was because of the cameras.

Her mother had put on such a show, India didn't protest when they suggested they go out to dinner to celebrate her "resurrection". Thank God, Aunt Val had been there, otherwise it would have been an even more trying ordeal.

The moment they sat down, her mother's mask slipped. "So, India, I see being on the island has done you some good. You were starting to get a little chubby."

Aunt Val glared at her sister. "Shut up, Leila. The girl had a wonderful shape. You only wish you looked as good as she did when you were her age."

Leila Powers had ignored her sister's comment and returned her attention to India. "And what did you do to your hair? Did you have to get it cut so short? You look like a little boy."

India thumbed through the menu, past the point of caring about what barbs came her way. Her future was secure, and in a few weeks, she'd be reunited with her men. There was nothing they could do to bring her down. Or so she had thought. "Mom, I was on an island without any hair care products or so much as a comb. My hair was a tangled mess. The hairdresser did the best she could, and I actually like this short do. It's easy to maintain." She ran her hands over her now shorn locks.

"I think it's cute," Aunt Val agreed with her. "It makes her look sophisticated. Would you stop picking on the girl?"

Leila looked at her sister with surprise. "Picking on her? Can't a mother give her daughter a little constructive criticism? Besides, Jack isn't so sensitive. Lord knows, I don't know how I could have two children so different from each other."

India pressed her lips to a thin line, clenching her teeth together, to bite back the retort on the tip of her tongue.

The mention of his son brought Trevor into the conversation. "Jack got a new job with an investment firm. He's on his way up. That boy is ambitious, and God help anyone who stands in his way."

Aunt Val snorted. "Isn't that what you said about his last four jobs? That boy can't stay in a job to save his life."

Trevor glared. "Valerie, if you're going to be so disagreeable, you shouldn't have joined us for dinner."

Her aunt would not back down. "If I recall correctly, my niece asked me to pick her up from the airport. It was you and Leila who insisted on coming out even though your daughter is bone weary. Did you think the cameras would follow us? Is that why you decided to magnanimously offer to treat us to dinner?"

India knew her aunt's heart was in the right place, but the more she defended her, the more it it made things worse. "Please, Aunt Val. Let's just have a nice dinner."

Val gave her a questioning look and India shook her head, pleading with her to let it go. She didn't want her first night back to end in an argument.

"That's sensible of you, India," her father said, "for once." The last shot was muttered under his breath, but she heard it all the same.

Her aunt looked as though she would say something, but India grabbed her hand and gave it a squeeze.

"I have my moments," India answered back. She was thankfully spared a reply when the waitress came by.

Just as India was about to give her order, the waitress interrupted her. "Aren't you the lady who was stuck on the island for two months?"

India smiled uneasily, wishing her fifteen minutes of fame would hurry up and be over with. "Yes, that's me."

"Oh, my gosh," the blonde gushed. "I saw your interview on the *Ann Webster Show*. It's pretty amazing how you survived on the island. I'm so jealous of you for spending all that time alone on a deserted island with those two hunks. How did you manage to keep your hands off of them?"

India's cheeks burned, and she lowered her head, hoping

her expression wouldn't give her away. If she only knew. She wasn't sure what to say to that, especially considering what did happen on that island.

"Young lady, that is a highly inappropriate comment and I suggest you keep these comments to yourself before we call the manager." Leila glared at the furiously blushing waitress.

India shot the blonde a sympathetic glance. Yes, her comment had been on the unprofessional side, but it wasn't so bad as to earn her mother's sharp condemnation. "It's okay. The waitress didn't mean anything by it, I'm sure."

"I really didn't, and I apologize if I offended you."

India waved her hand dismissively. "Think nothing of it."

After taking their orders, the waitress scurried away without a backward glance, and then her mother went on a tirade. "The nerve of the insolent girl. How dare she act so familiar to a patron! Not even India would do something so nasty as that woman implied." Leila turned and frowned, scrunching up her nose to emphasize her disgust.

That statement hit India where it hurt. Nasty? "What do you mean by that mom?"

"I don't need to dignify that question with a response, India Rochelle. I only hope other people don't get that same disgusting idea."

A mischievous grin curled her aunt's lips. "I don't know. That Puerto Rican one was pretty sexy. The blond wasn't hard on the eyes either."

India who had been in the process of taking a sip of water spit it out, spilling it all over the table.

"That's enough, Valerie. Your jokes are not appreciated. India may not have much sense, but we taught her better than that. Sometimes, I can't believe we're sisters."

Valerie laughed. "I think the same thing myself."

Leila chose to ignore that statement. The meal had gone from bad to worse, with her mother picking at her about how dark India had gotten in all that sun, to how inconvenient it had been to put all her things in storage when her landlords had contacted them.

By the end of dinner, India was nearly in tears. All her resolve to not let them affect her had crumbled. The barbs that had stung the most were the ones about Rafe and Grant, saying how awful it must have been for India to be on the island with two men who were obviously so beneath her.

She wanted to defend them and say how wrong her parents were, but all of her old insecurities came back full strength. India couldn't remember what it was she'd eaten, it could have been sawdust for all she knew, but it took all of her strength to not burst into tears.

Thankfully, they didn't insist she come home with them, when her aunt offered to take India back to her house.

She had spent the past week relaxing, at Aunt Val's insistence. India supposed she should follow through on the plans she'd made with Rafe and Grant, but something held her back.

India was so deep in thought, she didn't hear the footsteps approach.

"Hey, sweetie, wanna come help me with these groceries?" Aunt Val called from the kitchen entrance.

India smiled, glad for the company. "Sure." She went into the kitchen and began to unpack the food, while her Aunt went back outside to retrieve more bags.

She was putting things away when her aunt returned. "You shouldn't have bought all my favorite foods."

"Think nothing of it. Besides, we have to put a little meat back on your bones. You're still gorgeous as ever, but if you lose any more weight, you're going to make Nicole Ritchie look like a fatso."

India laughed. "I'm not that skinny."

Her aunt eyed her up and down. "When I saw you at the airport, I wanted to give you a sandwich. Now stop arguing. Didn't anyone ever tell you not to argue with your elders?"

"Well, if you continue to cook for me the way you have, then I'll have no problem putting weight back on."

They finished putting the remainder of the groceries away together, and India took the kettle out, filled it with water and placed it on the stove, knowing her aunt liked having her tea after a long day's work.

Val sighed, taking a seat at the kitchen table. "You're a doll. Can I keep you?"

India sat across from her. "I think you'll get tired of me after a while, besides, I have to sort out my work situation. I knew they wouldn't hold my job with no word from me, but the starting over again is a little depressing. I know you don't make a lot of money as a public defender and yes, I know some of my clients were guilty as sin, but for those few kids who may have gotten caught up in the wrong crowd, or made stupid mistakes—that's the part about my job that I miss. I liked helping those people turn their lives around. I knew their names and I cared about every single one of them."

"I know you did, baby. You have a good heart."

"My parents think I was stupid to take such a low paying job."

"Who cares what they think? Your parents are idiots."

"But they are my parents."

"It doesn't necessarily mean they're good at it. Stop worrying about what they think and do what makes you happy. Maybe you could work with legal aide or do some pro bono work."

"Actually, I was thinking about moving." India wanted to gauge her aunt's reaction to her declaration.

Val frowned. "What do you mean? Where would you go? You've lived in this area all your life?"

"And that's why I need a change. Can...can I ask you a personal question."

"Sure, honey. You know you can ask me anything."

She licked her lips before broaching the subject that had been plaguing her mind since her first dinner back. "Did you agree with Mom about what she said?"

Her aunt lifted a perfectly arched brow. "There's a lot I don't agree on with your mother. You'd have to be more specific, sweetie."

"At dinner, she was...upset when that waitress made the comment about not being able to keep her hands off of Rafe and Grant. Mom seemed to think it was wrong."

"Oh." Val frowned before understanding dawned. "Ooooohhh. Did something happen on your island with the three of you?"

"You answer my question first."

"Well...I wouldn't call it gross, but certainly unconventional. I will say this, however, if Denzel Washington and Jaime Foxx slid in my bed, I wouldn't kick them out. Now that I think about it, what woman wouldn't want to have two hunks in her bed?"

"Apparently my mother," India said dryly.

"Your mother has a stick up her ass. So now, answer my

question. Did something happen on the island between the three of you?"

India closed her eyes briefly. "Yes."

"Hmm, I thought I noticed a chemistry there during that interview, but I thought I was imagining things. What happened?"

She knew she could tell her aunt anything, but would she understand what those men meant to her. Would she think her disgusting and crazy for feeling the way she did about them? The last thing she wanted was her aunt's disapproval. She was India's only ally besides Rafe and Grant. If Aunt Val condemned her, it would be upsetting.

India took a deep breath and spilled everything, from the very beginning when she'd met them in the airport and noted her initial attraction to them, to the point where she discovered her love for them.

Val listened quietly until her niece was finished, her expression not giving anything away.

"So we made these plans to be together, but now that I'm back home, I'm scared. They're the best thing that's ever happened to me, but every serious relationship I've had has shattered to pieces. I can't help but wonder if this will be any different. It's almost like some greater force is telling me I don't have the right to be happy."

"Don't be silly, baby. You have every right to be happy. Yes, you've had some hard knocks in the relationship department, but it doesn't mean you won't be successful. You need to stop beating yourself up over the Kevin situation. If it was meant to be, he would have fought harder to keep you. Inside he retreated with his tail between his legs."

India hadn't thought of it that way. She had been beating herself up over the situation since she'd ended things. "I guess."

"And don't let me get started about Steven, the cheating son of a bitch. He didn't deserve you. You're better off without him. As for this thing... I don't really know what to make of it. Have you thought about your living arrangements? How you would introduce each other in public. Any possible children from this...threesome?"

"Well, we'd live together, and if there were children, we'd raise them together. The children would have two fathers."

"What? Now that sounds strange. Are these two men—"

"No, they're not bisexual. I told you, they're just close."

"Why?"

India had left out the part about their pasts. It wasn't her story to tell. "They just are. Please, Aunt Val, understand, these men make me happy."

"Right now, because you're starved for love, but the three of you were on a deserted island. You could be forgiven for doing what you did. I don't blame you or them, but I think you're being a little unrealistic if you don't think there will be complications."

Thankfully, the kettle began to whistle, giving India an excuse to leave the table. She fixed a cup of tea for her aunt and placed it on the table.

Val frowned. "Aren't you going to join me?"

"Actually, I think I'm going to take a walk. I need to clear my head."

Val grabbed her wrist when India would have walked past her. "I didn't mean to give you a hard time, but I'm only thinking of your well-being. I don't want to see you hurt, sweetie. And this could be an explosive situation."

"I know you're only saying this because you care, and I'm not mad at you." She bent over and gave Val a kiss on her

145

cheek to show there were no hard feelings.

She couldn't be angry at her aunt. How could she, when these were the same doubts that had been assailing her mind since they were rescued?

Chapter Fourteen

Rafe tried to concentrate on what was being said in the meeting. This past week seemed to be a parade of consecutive meetings. There was a lot for them to catch up on after being gone for so long. His head throbbed and all he wanted to do was retreat to his office and call India.

He missed her so much it hurt. Every night when he went to bed, he held his pillow tightly against his body, wishing it was her. He'd wake up with his body drenched in sweat, and his cock painfully hard. Whenever he talked to her on the phone, his ache only increased. Hearing her sweet voice only reminded him of how much he needed her in his life.

The problem was, the last time they'd spoke, she seemed distracted, and what was worse, she'd ended the call saying she had to go after only ten minutes. Grant had mentioned her being distant when they spoke on the phone, and Rafe began to worry.

He'd been so certain of her feelings for them. When they'd been on the island, she seemed happy enough to go along with their plans. Now he was beginning to have doubts. The last thing he wanted to think about was her changing her mind.

Was it the media attention they were still getting? He and Grant were still receiving calls about interviews. They were even contacted by a publisher to talk about a book deal. Rafe wanted it all to go away.

"Rafe!" Bill Jensen, the company's vice-president, snapped his fingers to get Rafe's attention.

"Huh?"

"Where did you go? I asked you a question about the Harlow project and who you wanted the point person to be on it. Grant thinks Mac may be a good candidate. I'm fine with that. What do you think?"

"I think we need to adjourn this meeting until later this afternoon. My head is killing me and I can barely see," he answered honestly.

Bill huffed. "Fine. But we really need to get this settled. How about we try this again at three?"

Bill reported directly to him, and since he'd come back, he sensed the other man's resentment. When he and Grant had been gone, Bill was in charge. Maybe it was time to make Bill partner. After all, he'd proved his worth time and time again.

"Three will be fine. I really appreciate all you've done."

Bill nodded before leaving the room.

Grant remained in his chair. "Do you really have a headache?"

The side of his mouth tilted. "Not as bad as I made it out to be, but I really didn't hear a word he said."

Grant stroked his chin. "I had a hell of a time concentrating myself. It's killing you too isn't it?"

"More than you know."

"Oh, I have an idea. I should have listened to you when you voiced your concerns about India earlier, but I was so sure."

"Don't tell me you're giving up on her."

"Hell no. But I think we need to reassess the situation. Maybe she's been influenced by other people's opinions. Last night it was almost as if she couldn't wait to get off the phone with me, yet when I called she seemed glad I did. These mixed signals are frustrating."

"I'm thinking we should pay her a visit and remind her just how good we are together."

Rafe liked that idea a lot. "I like the way you think. We should—"

The door flew open and Rafe's assistant walked in. "Rafe, you have a visitor and she says she won't go away until she sees you."

"Gee, Amy, knock much?" Rafe asked sarcastically.

She placed her hands on her hips. "Don't play the heavy-handed boss now. I wouldn't have interrupted if it wasn't important. I think you'd better come out now and see who it is. They're waiting in your office. It's not a reporter, by the way."

"Then who the hell is it?"

"Why don't you just see for yourself?" She turned around and then left the room.

Rafe groaned. "I don't know why I put up with that woman."

Grant chuckled. "Because, despite her smart mouth, she's good at her job."

"Lucky for her that she is. I'd better go see who it is. I hope it's not a reporter."

He wondered who it could be as he made his way to his office. When Rafe opened the door, he thought his eyes were playing tricks on him. Perched on his desk, examining her nails with a bored expression on her face, was his ex-wife.

The last time he'd seen her was in court and the words

they'd exchanged hadn't been pleasant.

When he entered the room, she lifted her head, her red-painted lips tilted into a feline smile. She looked like the cat who'd swallowed the cream. Since he'd last seen her, she'd dyed her hair from ash blonde to platinum, and her breasts looked bigger than he remembered, and her lips looked like she'd been stung by a hive of bees, although Rafe had a feeling that was the look she was going for.

A lot of guys would have found her alterations a turn-on, but when he looked at her, all Rafe felt was disgust. After being with India, he almost felt unclean for having touched her. The suffocating scent of her overpowering perfume filled the air and made his stomach turn.

"Hello, Rafe."

"So I see this is where the settlement money has gone."

She patted her big hair. Angie always did like to wear it bigger than he liked. He used to attribute that to her being from South Jersey. "Do you like what you see?"

"You look...different."

She laughed, a fake tinkling sound. "I get lots of compliments. Most people think I look like a life-sized Barbie."

That was rich. "Only if they make Trailer Park Barbie."

Angie pouted though she seemed unperturbed. "That isn't nice, especially when I've come by for a friendly visit."

He wasn't in the mood to play games with her. She was up to something. "Cut the crap, Angie. Let's not pretend you don't have an ulterior motive for coming here."

She dropped her jaw in mock surprise. "Moi? Really, Rafe, you always were paranoid. I came to see how you were doing after your trying experience. I know we parted ways on not so amicable terms, but that doesn't mean I don't still care about you."

"But it certainly means I don't care for you and haven't for a very long time. Nor will I stand here exchanging pleasantries with you, when I'd rather see you in hell."

"I was only trying to be nice."

"You've never been nice, unless you wanted something."

She tossed her hair over her shoulders, her lips firming in her annoyance. There was once time he found her very attractive and could think of nothing else but possessing her. Now Rafe couldn't for the life of him think why that was. "I saw you and your friend on television. I'm sorry to hear about your ordeal."

"Angie..." he growled in warning, wishing she'd get to the point.

"I'm just expressing my sympathy; can't I at least do that? Anyway, I thought it was interesting that there were three of you on the island. Your little friend, Iris, or was her name Ingrid? Well, it doesn't matter. How did she get on with you two?"

"What are you getting at?" he demanded.

"She's very pretty. I could understand if something might have happened between the three of you. After all, you guys were stranded on a deserted island and you're all virile attractive people, so naturally...it wouldn't be a stretch for people to assume that something might have happened, sexually I mean."

He knew where she was going with this, and he wanted to wring her neck. "Angie, if you've come here to make threats..."

She chuckled. "Rafe, you should know me well enough to remember I don't make threats. I just thought I'd warn you that with all your recent attention in the news, people might start delving into your past and as your ex-wife I may be contacted...or maybe I could offer the reporters some information." Malice glistened in her eyes. "We did have an interesting sex life, didn't we, Raphael. How's Grant, by the way?"

"Get out of this office before I strangle you with my bare hands."

She lifted a brow. "Oh, come on, Rafe. You wouldn't want to do something so foolish. Besides, how do you think your new little friend would hold up under the scrutiny?"

Rafe knew Grant wouldn't care if Angie went to the press about their past relationship, but he didn't want to expose India to what the people would say, viewing what they shared as something negative and perverted.

Angie must have known she had him by the balls because she revealed large white teeth. "Sweetie, it doesn't have to come to that point of course. I could come down with a case of amnesia."

"What do you want?" he bit out through clenched teeth. He'd never been more close to hitting a woman than he was in that moment.

"Oh, a nice check would make me forget. You were awful stingy with the settlement."

"What the fuck are you talking about? You got a more than generous amount, more than your cheating ass deserved."

She shrugged. "I guess we'll have to agree to disagree. I want fifty thousand dollars, from you and...the same amount from Grant."

He balled his fists together at his sides. "And how long do we have before you get the money?"

"I'm not an unreasonable person. I'll give you two weeks. I

want it wired to my account. I'll forward you my details in a couple days." She slid off the desk and sauntered over to him with a triumphant smile.

"Once you get your damn money, I don't ever want to see you again. If I do, I think I'll kill you."

She patted him on the cheek with condescension. "I knew you'd be sensible about this, hon." Angie ran her fingertip down the length of his torso and didn't seem like she'd stop her descent.

Rafe caught her hand just before it touched his crotch. "Keep your hands off of me, bitch."

She laughed. "You used to like my touch."

"I used to do a lot of things that weren't good for me. Now get the hell out of here while you're still able."

Angie must have seen something in his eyes because she backed away, but it didn't erase the sneer on her face. "Just have my money by the deadline, if you want to avoid any unnecessary embarrassments." She moved past him then and left the office, leaving Rafe seething.

8∽

India sat at her aunt's computer updating her resume. She was normally a fast and accurate typist, but she kept making mistakes every other word. Cursing in frustration, she knew it was no use when she was so distracted. She saved the document and shut down the terminal, then stood up and stretched.

The conversation she'd had with Val the day before was still plaguing her mind. Knowing what her aunt thought put things into a different perspective. She'd asked practical questions that had India wondering if there was some validity to those points.

No matter how much she mulled it over in her mind however, she still missed Rafe and Grant. Every night before she fell asleep, they were her last thought and when she woke in the morning they were the first people on her mind. Talking on the phone with them wasn't enough. She found herself cutting their conversations short because it was too hard to hear their voices and not be there.

She couldn't imagine what they would be thinking. Were they thinking about her and how often? Did her absence make their hearts grow fonder, or did it make them wander. Worse still, even though she couldn't be more in love with anyone as she was with those two, she began to doubt if she was the right woman for them.

Maybe she wasn't strong enough to be their woman, to deal with the lifestyle. She'd always think that they'd grow tired of her and move on, that she'd end up getting hurt somehow.

India was on the way to the kitchen to get something to drink when the telephone rang. Val was at work so it was either for her or a telemarketer. She looked at the phone and was surprised to see that the number belonged to her parents.

She picked up the receiver and placed it against her ear. "Hello?"

"India. I'm so glad you're there," her mother greeted, actually sounding genuinely pleased.

"Hi, Mom. How are you today?" she asked, bracing herself for the scathing comments to come.

"I was calling because your father and I are having a little get together at the house this Sunday, just a small dinner really, and we'd like for you to come."

India sighed. "I'm not really in much of a mood for company. If you don't mind, I think I'll pass." Plus she didn't
154

think she was up to dealing with a round of taunts and innuendoes from her parents.

"Please, India. We've invited a very important guest and we already said you would be there."

"Why did you say that? I could have had plans?"

"Jack is coming home this weekend. I would think you'd at least want to see your brother."

She didn't want to in particular. Jack was just as verbally abusive as her parents except his comments were never subtle and always meant to cause the maximum amount of pain. "Mom, I'll just have to see him another time."

"Listen, you little ingrate. I went to a lot of trouble to get this dinner party together, and you will show up. This is no longer a request." Leila's words came out like a harsh command.

There was the woman India knew so well. "And if I don't?" she challenged.

"Don't be stupid. Be there at seven. No earlier and no later. And wear something nice." Her mother hung up without giving her a chance to answer.

The sad thing was, India knew she'd end up going.

Chapter Fifteen

Grant clutched the wheel in a near death grip as he tried to concentrate on the road. Almost there. In a few more minutes they would see India again. He'd called her the night before to say they would be down. Not able to go another night without seeing her, without being with her, he and Rafe agreed to make a visit.

After the week they had, this was a much needed get away. Besides, she needed to be warned about Angie. He couldn't trust that woman as far as he could throw her, and even if they did give her the money, there was no guarantee she'd keep quiet. And who was to say she wouldn't want more, and they would have to keep paying. The money wasn't the issue. He'd gladly do it to get the bitch off his back and to ensure India didn't come under fire.

"You haven't said anything for the past hour. What's on your mind?" Rafe broke into his thoughts.

"Probably the same thing that's running through yours. I still can't believe she would pull a stunt like this. She's a snake, but I never thought she'd stoop so low."

"Believe it. That woman is rotten to the core. I can't think of one redeeming quality about her."

Grant nodded in agreement. "It actually makes me sick to my stomach that I once wanted her."

"You and me both. After she left my office, I had the cleaning crew come in to wipe the office down. It stank of her perfume. She spends money like it's going out of style. Even when we were married, Angie was draining me dry. It wouldn't surprise me if she's gone through her settlement already. Too bad she hasn't conned another sucker into paying for her expensive tastes."

"I don't mind about the money, but my fear is she'll keep coming back for more, not to mention the fact she may get to India somehow."

Rafe slammed his fist against the dashboard, his body shaking with visible anger. "If she fucking goes near India, it will be the last thing she does."

"Easy, Rafe. When you told me what Angie was up to, I wanted to kill her myself, but there has got to be some way to thwart her. India has to be warned."

Rafe shook his head. "No. I don't want her to know. We can handle this ourselves, there's no need to make her worry unnecessarily."

"I understand your line of thinking, but if we're all going to share our lives together, it's only fair she be made aware of what's going on. Somehow, I don't think she'd appreciate us keeping something like this from her."

Rafe slumped in his seat, his lips drooped into a frown. "I guess you're right, but exactly how do we broach a subject like this? Everything will be wonderful with us, but by the way, my psycho ex-wife may pop up every now and then to demand money or else she'll expose us. It's my hope that if we just give her the money now, by the time she comes around asking for more, no one will give two shits about us anymore. I can think of a lot of people who gained notoriety some way or another who haven't been heard from in years. We just happen to be the flavor of the month right now."

Grant picked up the directions on the dash and gave them a quick once over before returning his attention back to the road. According to these directions they were less than a mile away. "I understand your line of reasoning, but she still needs to know."

"I know. But what if bringing this up opens a new can of worms?"

"What do you mean?" Grant maneuvered his car down a narrow residential street.

"From the last few conversations you've had with her, do you get the impression she might be looking for an excuse to sever ties with us? Imagine what she'd say if we told her about this. It could be the thing to make her do just that."

Grant stole a look at his friend. "I'm surprised to hear you say that? You've always been the one who's been so sure about everything working out."

"Of course I have worries, but I never saw any point in bringing them up. It's only this past week, being away from her, that's made me wonder if she might have been using us for emotional support on the island."

"You know India isn't like that. What we had on the island was real, as were her feelings, but you forget, she's back on her own turf now dealing with the issues she's left behind. We've had years to deal with what happened to us growing up, and we had each other. She had no one. When someone has dealt with what she has all her life, it isn't so easy to change all your ideas. The prospect of her trying to pull away from us frightens me too, but we can't stop believing in her love for us just because we've faced the first road bump in our relationship."

Rafe sighed. "I guess you're right."

Grant turned on Maple Street and looked for number 716.

It was two houses down. He pulled over to the curb and shut off the engine in front of a small brick house. "Here we are."

"There's a couple of cars in the driveway, but I'm not sure if one of them is hers. I know this is her aunt's house, but I don't know how many people live here."

Grant took the keys out of the ignition and opened the door. "I believe her aunt is single, or at least I think that's what she said. What are we waiting for? Let's go? I can't wait to see her."

It was three rings before the door was answered. An attractive woman, who looked to be in her late twenties to early thirties, answered the door. She seemed hesitant at first, but then a slow smile curved her lips. "You must be Rafe and Grant. I remember seeing you on television but India has told me so much about you, I already feel like you're old friends. Come on in." She stood back to open the door wide enough for them to enter.

Rafe extended his hand once he was inside. "And you must be Aunt Valerie. I can tell that good looks must run in this family."

Her caramel cheeks reddened to a becoming blush. "You're a smooth one aren't you? Please call me Val." She took the hand offered to her and gave it a shake before turning to Grant. "And it's very nice to meet you as well, Grant."

He smiled as he shook her hand. "It's my pleasure." Grant looked around the room, wondering where India was.

"My niece is upstairs trying to pretty herself up, although I told her she looked fine. Now I can see why she's going through all the trouble. The cameras didn't do you two justice." She gave them both an appreciative smile.

Grant grinned. He liked this woman. She had the type of personality that immediately put people at ease. He certainly

159

needed it when his nerves were already frazzled. "India never told us her aunt was so young and beautiful."

"Hardly young. I'm pushing forty, but unfortunately I can't attribute my youthful features to good clean living. I guess it must be genetics." She gestured them further inside her living room. "Please have a seat, and India should be down shortly. May I offer you a drink? I have Sam Adams, Coke, lemonade, orange juice and water."

"A beer would be great." Rafe smiled gratefully.

"I'll just have water please."

She nodded her head. "Gotcha. One beer, one water. I'll be back in a minute."

"She's nice," Rafe observed.

"Yes. India is lucky she at least has one relative in her life who cares for her."

"I'm very lucky to have Aunt Val," India said softly as she entered the room. She'd moved with such stealth and grace, neither he or Rafe had heard her approach.

Both men stood. Grant's heart did a summersault as he drank in her beauty. She wore a pink tank top that skimmed the gentle swell of her breasts and a khaki mini-skirt that showed off her shapely legs. Her short haircut sat well with her, making India's brown eyes look bigger than ever and her cheekbones higher.

She gave them a tentative smile. "I'm glad you two came. I..." India broke off, stared at them for a minute, before launching herself toward them.

Grant caught her in his arms, holding her tight and not wanting to let go. Rafe moved behind her and molded himself against her back.

"I missed the two of you so much. It almost seems surreal

to have you here right now. It was one thing to talk to you on the phone, but your being in plain sight is so much better than I imagined." She sighed.

Grant couldn't tear his gaze away from her upturned face. "I don't remember you being this beautiful, or maybe you just got even lovelier." When he would have taken her lips in a kiss, he halted at the sound of a throat clearing broke him out of his trance.

"Sorry to break up the reunion, but I have your drinks." Val reentered the room. She looked at each of them in turn as though trying to assess the situation. How much had India told her about what happened on the island, and furthermore, did she approve?

Whether she did or not, she didn't give any indication. Grant supposed she would be a bit curious, but he wasn't going to offer any explanation when none was demanded. Reluctantly, he let go of India, as did Rafe.

India moved away from them, smoothing her clothing with her hands. "Aunt Val, I take it you've met Grant and Rafe?"

Val came forward and handed Grant his drink with a smile. "Yes, we've met. You never told me how charming they were."

Grant took a seat with drink in hand and took a sip. India sat on the couch next to him and Rafe on the opposite side of her. He shifted uncomfortably in his seat from her closeness. His cock stirred and he willed it to stay down, otherwise it would cause a bit of embarrassment. From the corner of his eye, he could tell Rafe was having a similar dilemma.

Val gave him a reassuring smile. "So how does it feel to be back in civilization? Are you having a hard time acclimating back into your lives?"

"It's been interesting. We're still trying to get used to the attention we're getting. This has certainly taught me to appreciate the little luxuries in life we take for granted, like clean running water, a fresh change of clothing and a hot meal. I don't think I ever want to see another fish again." Rafe made a face at the memory.

"So how long do you plan on staying?" Val asked.

"We'll be in the city for the weekend, and then we have to head back on Sunday. There's still a lot we need to sort out with our company," Grant explained.

"I hope you two aren't thinking of staying at a hotel. I have plenty of room here. I'd be happy to have you with us," Val offered.

"No!" India said sharply. "I mean...they can't." She wouldn't meet anyone's eyes.

Why would she say that? There was no doubt in Grant's mind that India had been glad to see them, so why now did she seem so anxious to drive them away. Whatever the deal was, he couldn't wait until he and Rafe could be alone with her and find out exactly what was going on with her mixed messages. "We would love to stay here, but we wouldn't want to inconvenience you."

Val reached over and patted him on the knee in a gesture of reassurance. "It's no trouble at all. India is just being silly. Of course you can stay. I love visitors, and any friends of my niece are friends of mine. Besides, offering you a place to crash for the weekend is the least I can do. From what India has told me, if it wasn't for you two, she wouldn't have made it. Please say you'll stay."

"Thank you. We will." Rafe gave India a narrowed-eyed look, daring her to protest.

"Then it's all settled."

India nibbled on her bottom lip, still not looking at anyone in particular.

Grant bent his head a couple inches from her ear. "Are you okay, India?"

"Yes. I'm fine. I...it's nothing." She eyed her aunt. "Aunt Val, didn't you want me to remind you that you have to pick up that thing you wanted by..." she glanced at her watch, "...six?"

The bewilderment on the other woman's face made it quite clear to Grant there was no thing she needed to get, but India's excuse to get rid of her. "What thing?"

"Don't you remember? That thing you couldn't stop talking about. You were very adamant about me reminding you about it."

Comprehension soon dawned in the woman's hazel eyes. "Oh yeah. *That thing.* I almost forgot about it. Thank you for reminding me. I'll run out and get it." She hopped up and gave them an apologetic smile. "I'm sorry I have to run like that. I was hoping I'd get to cook something for you boys, but India can pop something in the oven for you. I'll be back later tonight."

When Val left the house, no one said a word until they saw from the window her little Jeep pulling out of the driveway.

Grant crossed his arms over his chest, turning his gaze toward a fidgeting India. "How about telling us what the hell is going on."

India realized they must believe she was being schizoid, but in her mind she had a very good reason for them not staying here the night. "I just thought it would be better for us if the two of you stayed in the hotel for the weekend." She stood and began to pace the room, putting as much distance between them as she possibly could, but when she was near them, India couldn't think properly.

Rafe stood up as well and strode across the room, not

163

giving her any quarter. "Why the hell not? Didn't you want us to come this weekend?"

"I did. I missed you two and wanted to see you again, but I didn't want you to stay here at my aunt's house."

Amber eyes glistened dangerously. "Well we're here, and you're not going to be able to dismiss us so easily as you have on the telephone." He put his arms around her waist and covered her mouth with his before she could utter a protest.

Just like every other time they kissed, her pussy tingled in arousal. India didn't have the strength to resist him. She twined her hands through his dark waves, holding his face to hers. Her nipples puckered until they were painfully sensitive peaks, straining against the material of her shirt.

Her tongue danced around his as she surrendered to the heat infusing her body. India's pulse raced, and she rejoiced in being in Rafe's arms again. The week had felt like a year being without them.

It was Rafe who broke the kiss. "Now how can you still have any doubts after that? Your body is begging for it." Without warning, he lifted her skirt and inserted his fingers into her panties.

India's gasp of surprise swiftly turned into one of wicked desire.

Rafe removed his hands from her panties to reveal their moisture. "You see? Your pussy is wet, and I bet you want to be fucked right here and now."

She would have looked stupid to deny the obvious. "I do want you both. The only reason I didn't want you to stay here was because I was hoping I could go back to the hotel with you. There's nothing I want more right now than to spend time with you...but I don't want it to be under the watchful eye of my aunt. She means well, but she can be a bit overprotective of me at times. We wouldn't be able to..." India lowered her eyes.

Rafe groaned. "Oh, baby. I'm sorry. We jumped to the wrong conclusion. It wouldn't have been something you wanted to bring up in front of Val."

She chuckled. "Definitely not."

Grant made his way across the room to them. "Hey, where's my kiss? I think I deserve one after putting up with this grouch on the ride down."

India moved away from Rafe and threw her arms around Grant with an upturned face, eager to receive his kiss. "Of course."

Grant's kiss was slow and unhurried. He took his time with it, gliding his tongue across the seam of her lips. "Delicious. I don't know how I lasted the week without doing that," he muttered before pressing his mouth firmly over hers again. He slid his hands down her back to cup her bottom, grinding his erection against the juncture of her thighs.

Grant squeezed her ass, pulling her closer against him. Suddenly he lifted her along the length of his body, and India, so in tune with his needs knew what he wanted from her without saying a word. She wrapped her legs around his waist which resulted in her skirt riding over her hips.

So caught up with the way he made her feel, India didn't notice he'd moved until her back was against the living room wall. He gyrated his hips against her pelvis, humping her, and pressing her breasts flat with the hardness of his taut torso.

Even though her aunt knew what had happened with the three of them on the island, out of respect for her, India had decided that if anything happened this weekend when she, Rafe and Grant got together, it wouldn't happen under her aunt's roof.

More than anything she wanted to rip their clothes off and

fuck both of them on the floor, but reason took over. She broke off the kiss, turning her head away as she tried to gain her breath.

India rested her head against Grant's shoulders. "Wow."

"Wow is right." Grant sounded as if he too was having trouble getting his breathing back to a normal cadence.

Untwining her legs from his waist, she let her feet touch the floor as she moved down his body. "I want to make love, but not here."

Rafe ran his fingers along the nape of her neck. "We'll take you out to dinner, and then check into a hotel room. There's no need to bring more than a toothbrush because you're not going to need any clothes."

Chapter Sixteen

A big dollop of chili fell on her chin as she took a hearty bite of her chili cheese dog. This was her third one and at the rate she was going, she'd probably have another.

Grant took a sip from his cup, giving her a look of indulgent amusement. "You're really putting those things away."

Rafe grinned. "You must have a hollow leg to eat like that. I have to admit, it's refreshing to take a beautiful woman out and see her actually enjoy her meal, although I wish we could have taken you someplace nicer than Hot Dog Heaven."

"Are you kidding?" she asked with her mouth full. "This place is great. When I was in law school, I lived off of these things, especially when I had to study for an important exam. I'd inhale them."

"I guess it's not so bad, once you get past the circus decoration and the sinister looking clown statue in the corner." Grant laughed.

"It's called atmosphere. Don't tell me you're a restaurant snob."

Rafe grinned. "I'm not that at all, let's just say I prefer a place where our food isn't severed in colorful cardboard boxes," he teased.

She poked her tongue out at him. India hadn't felt this relaxed in a long time. She'd missed the easy conversation and the camaraderie she shared with them. Her only regret was they'd go back home when the weekend was over, but while it lasted she wanted to make the most of it.

She popped the last bit of food into her mouth and wiped her lips and chin with the napkin. "I...I think I owe the two of you an apology."

Rafe cocked his head to the side? "Why?"

"For the way I acted on the phone this past week. I know it sounded like I was brushing you off or that I may have been a little standoffish, but I've had a lot on my mind since I've returned. It's a stressful situation when one decides to pack up and move from the one area they've know all their lives. When you guys went back home, everything on the island felt like a dream. I wanted to be with you so much that sometimes it was too painful to remain on the line with either one of you. I know it may sound stupid, but it's how I felt."

"That's not stupid—"

"No you're not—"

Both men began to talk at the same time and stopped, and then they were all laughing.

"You first," Grant offered.

Rafe reached across the table and took her hand in his. "India, I don't think you were stupid at all. It actually warms my heart to know your feelings are as strong for us as ours are for you. I know this can't be an easy situation, but sometimes it's better to share what's on your mind. If you have any doubts, never let one of them be that we don't love you."

"I know. I love you both too, but..." What she had to say was interrupted when a woman with big, bright-red hair walked over to their table.

"Didn't I see the three of you on television?" she said in a loud booming voice which drew the stares of some of the other patrons.

Grant looked annoyed, and Rafe didn't seem any happier. India hadn't been out much other than to run a couple of errands for her aunt, so this was the first time she'd been recognized since that dinner with her parents.

Realizing that neither man was interested in answering the question, India crossed her fingers beneath the table. "I don't think so."

The woman pursed her lips and placed her hands on her hips. "Oh, no. I did see you on television. You were the three survivors of that plane crash and you survived on an island by eating bugs and crap like that. I couldn't have done that. I would have rather starved."

India shrugged. "When faced with starvation, you'd be surprised what you'll eat."

"Not me. I wouldn't do it," the woman persisted.

She really wasn't in the mood to have a discussion of this random person's eating habits. "Well, I guess we all have ways of handling things."

"Why didn't you just catch fish?"

India's eyes crossed. Why wasn't she going away?

"We did eat fish, but we weren't able to catch them every day. It's much easier said than done." Grants spoke tight-lipped.

The woman laughed. "I wouldn't have left the water until I caught a fish."

"Well, it's too bad you weren't on the island with us then, it would have saved us from eating bugs." India's patience was slowly starting to ebb away.

"I just might of, but I wouldn't have been in that situation to begin with. I don't fly. Just don't trust those things, no siree. I'd prefer to have my feet planted firmly on the ground."

"Good for you," India muttered.

The redhead went on unperturbed, eyeing Rafe and Grant like they were slabs of meat at the delicatessen. "So how did the three of you spend your nights? I bet you guys had to get really cozy didn't you? I sure wouldn't have minded that part."

India could tell both men were about to explode. But she shook her head at them. It took everything within her to bite back the scathing retort on her tongue, but she managed to keep it to herself. "It was nice meeting you," she said instead, making it clear she wanted the woman to go away.

"I wanted to ask how you three went to the bath—"

"Rachael! Will you stop bugging these people?" A man appeared, saving them from being asked a way too personal question.

Rachael pouted. "I simply wanted to know if—"

The man had a look of long sufferance which told India this was probably her husband. The man should have been a candidate for sainthood. "I apologize for my wife harassing you." He took the redhead firmly by the hand and marched her off.

"I think it's time for us to get out of here," Grant suggested.

India nodded. She'd lost her appetite.

Once they were in the car, she rested her head against the window with a sigh. That woman had rattled her. She thought people would have been tired of their story by now, but that wasn't apparently so.

"If you hadn't been there, I would have told that woman where to go," Rafe said from the back seat.

"And what good would that have done? She probably would

have gotten louder, drawing more attention to us and then she might have even caused a scene. Frankly, that's something I could have done without."

Grant maneuvered the car out of the parking lot. "You're right, but I was very close to losing it myself."

What bothered India the most was the innuendo Rachael had made about the three of them? It wasn't the first time someone had intimated that something probably happened with the three of them. She could only imagine what other people were thinking who weren't brazen enough to voice their opinion. Again she wondered how their relationship would look to the outside world. Before they'd been rudely interrupted in the restaurant, she was about to express her concerns about their plans. On the island, everything had sounded lovely and idealistic. But now they were back, she wondered how practical their arrangement would be.

They'd spoken of children, and raising them together as one big happy family, but what would it be like for their kids to go to school and possibly deal with being made fun of because their family was different. And they'd never be able to show affection for one another in public without someone giving them a funny stare, and what about the people like Rachael who would make their thoughts known, no matter whether their opinions were warranted or not.

So lost in her thoughts, she didn't notice that they'd pulled into the hotel. India waited in the car, while the men checked in. When they returned, Grant drove them to the back entrance.

When they finally made it to the room, she noted the king-sized bed dominating the room. It was big enough for all of them. She took a seat on the edge with a sigh. "I'm so glad we can be alone finally."

Instead of joining her on the bed, Grant sat on the love seat adjacent to the bed, and Rafe on the chair in front of the desk. The mood had somehow changed and she wasn't sure why.

"Is something the matter?" she wanted to know.

The men looked at each other as she waited for one of them to speak.

"Well, is one of you going to talk?"

Rafe shifted in his chair with a look of discomfort. "I think there's something you should know."

"What?" She didn't like how this sounded and he hadn't even begun yet. Had they changed their minds? Did the two have doubts about this relationship?

"My ex-wife is trying to make trouble for me." Rafe balled his fists in his lap. His face went red in his anger.

"How? Does she want you back?" India asked, scared to hear the answer.

"Even if she did, that bitch wouldn't have a chance. No, what she wants is money. A lot of it."

"But if you're already divorced and she's received her settlement, then what's the problem?"

Rafe snorted. "I think I've already told you she has a cash register where her heart should be."

From what they'd told her about Rafe's ex-wife, she sounded like a nasty piece of work. India hoped they never met because she would probably give the woman a much deserved punch in the face. "Has she filed a motion in court? It's a long shot for her if she wants more money after signing the papers, but it's not unheard of. Is that what's happening?"

"No. She's not that smart, besides, if she did, Angie wouldn't get one red cent. Anyway, what use is the court to her when she's basically got us by the balls anyway?"

A chill crept into her system. "What do you mean?"

Rafe told her the details about his meeting with Angie. By the time he was finished relaying his story, she not only wanted to punch that heffa in the face, India wanted to administer an old school beat down.

"That's extortion! She can't do that."

"But she's doing it," Grant joined in the conversation.

"But it's not fair that she should demand money from the both of you."

Rafe stood up to pace the room. "I know this, but the woman is warped. I think this is her way to not only extract money from us, but get revenge. She didn't want the divorce. Angie's the kind of women who wants to be the ender of the relationship instead of the other way around. Obviously we didn't end on good terms and I had a few choice words for her she didn't appreciate."

India didn't quite know what to say. To have their relationship exposed to the world and possibly picked apart was her worst fear. India wasn't sure if she'd be able to handle the scrutiny, but she wouldn't stand by and let this woman get away with such a dirty trick. She'd rather take the heat from the public than allow that to happen.

"You can't give in to her demands. She'll keep coming back for money whenever she thinks she can get something out of you. I won't let you do it." She got off the bed, walked over to Rafe and cupped his face. "Don't do this out of some misguided attempt to protect me."

"India." Grant came up behind her and turned her to face him. "She's threatening to reveal the details of our marriage, and knowing her, she's not above embellishing details. Once that information is out, people will begin to speculate about the three of us."

"People are speculating about us now. Look at that woman

in the restaurant. Hers isn't the first innuendo I've dealt with."

Grant brushed her cheek with his knuckles. "Innuendo is one thing. But once Angie tells her tale, there will be more than pure speculation."

"I don't like the sound of this."

"What choice is there?" Rafe asked, his voice dripping with frustration.

"There's always a choice and you should choose not to give in to her blackmail."

"India, our minds are made up," Grant said with finality.

She put some distance between herself and them, needing to think. Plopping on the bed, India wondered again if she was strong enough to handle being with both of them in a lasting relationship.

"Your minds are made up, but shouldn't I have a say in this matter as well?"

Grant joined her on the bed and put his arm around her. "Which is why it has to be done. If it only affected me and Rafe, her threats wouldn't amount to shit, but realizing your concerns, we can't risk you getting hurt."

"Even if she did go to the media with details of her marriage to Rafe, the only news outfits who would be interested in a story like that would be the tabloids, and no one takes those seriously. Like Rafe said, people will soon lose interest in who we are."

Rafe shook his head. "It's still not a chance we're willing to take. Look, the only reason I brought this up in the first place was to give you a word of warning in case she somehow gets your information and contacts you. It may sound far-fetched, but I wouldn't put anything past her."

"Well, since you two are so determined to be my saviors, I

guess there's nothing really left to say."

Rafe walked over to the bed and sat on the other side of her. He ran his hand along her bare thigh. "There may be nothing left to say, but there is plenty left for us to do." He leaned over and gave her a kiss on the neck.

India didn't want the conversation to end, but they were just as determined that it should.

She turned her head away from his questing lips. "I'm not going to let you distract me."

Grant kissed India's exposed shoulder. "How long do you think you'll be able to resist us, when we all know you go crazy when we do this?" He cupped her breast and rubbed his thumb under her nipple.

She squirmed. Already she felt a warmth flickering within the pit of her belly and spreading to her entire body. "Mmm, you won't make me forget so easily."

Rafe ran his tongue along the shell of her ear. "What about this?"

"Ooh. That's not fair," she moaned.

Grant gently pushed her back on the bed and pulled her top off, while Rafe worked on her skirt. Once she was completely naked, they stood up and stripped. They both caressed her with such slow deliberate ease, she knew they were doing it on purpose.

"Are you two going to torment me like this for the rest of the night, or will you join me on the bed and fuck me?" Her mouth went dry at the sight of those two big cocks, hard and ready for her.

They slithered on the bed toward India until they were on either side of her. She lay on her back as two heads, one dark, one blond, moved to her breasts. Her nipples became alive beneath their mouths.

"Mmm, that feels lovely." She stroked the backs of their heads, letting her fingers trail down their necks. India couldn't keep still beneath their sensual ministrations, as they bathed her with their tongues.

"You have no idea how much I've been thinking about this." Grant sighed when he lifted his head to look at her, his blue eyes gleaming with stark possession.

India shook her head back and forth against the pillow with a throaty laugh. "Oh, but I do. I know exactly what you were going through, because I felt it too." She hadn't been this alive in days. The desolate ache and the uncertainty from being away from them no longer mattered. They were together now, the most important thing.

Rafe licked the side of her neck. "It's been torture without you, baby." He splayed his hand on her stomach and repositioned himself at her feet. Lifting one of her ankles, he kissed the heel of her foot and then her toes, before making an ascent up the length of her legs, stopping only when he reached her pussy.

Rafe dragged out the torture by kissing the insides of her thighs, as though he was deliberately avoiding her throbbing mons. Enflamed from his kisses she lifted her hips, demanding he give her what she wanted most. He laughed. "Patience, baby, I've been away from you for too long to rush this."

Grant gave her no time to reply when his mouth closed over hers. She wrapped her arms around his neck, and ran her fingers down his back, reveling in the savagery of his kiss. His tongue stabbed into her mouth, dominating and consuming her. Grant squeezed one of her breasts, grazing his thumb against her nipple.

India's toes curled as jolts of ecstasy shot through her

body, sliding along her nerve endings. She groaned into his mouth as her nails dug into his flesh. She couldn't get enough of what they were doing to her.

Her pussy pulsed in her need. Moisture wet the inside of her thighs. Rafe parted her legs further and finally brought his lips to her swollen labia. He spread the folds and stroked her heated flesh with the broad side of his tongue.

India nearly lost her mind when Rafe latched on to her pulsing button with his teeth. Bucking her hips, she mashed her box against his face. Giving in to her silent demand, he sucked her clit with voracious tugs.

She tore her mouth away from Grant's to catch her breath. "Oh...my...God," she gasped.

"He can't help you now," Grant growled, burying his face against her neck with urgent kisses. He squeezed her breasts hard, but India was too enraptured to feel anything but mind-boggling passion.

Rafe released her clit and stabbed her channel with his tongue, pushing it as deep as it would go into her pussy.

India didn't think she could take much more of this. She wanted those cocks inside of her right now! "Fuck me now!"

Grant slowly pulled away from her and slid off the bed.

"Where are you going?" she asked breathlessly.

"I need to get some lubrication, because I intend on getting some of that ass."

Rafe continued to fuck her with his tongue until she neared her orgasm. Her pussy gushed. She grabbed Rafe by the hair, pulling him away from her. "No. I need you inside of me now."

He chuckled, his amber eyes twinkling. "Okay, baby." He positioned himself until they were face to face.

She lifted her thighs to grant him access to her sex. Eager

to have him inside of her, India grabbed his dick and placed it against her pussy. "I need you now."

"Easy, baby. You'll have me." He moved his hand between their bodies, and parted her labia before thrusting into her channel.

India sighed with relief. The only thing to make this moment complete was to have both men inside of her. Rafe stroked the side of her thigh, waiting for Grant to rejoin them. They didn't have long to wait before Grant returned with the lubrication. She shivered when Grant rubbed the slick gel against her puckered ring. He pushed a finger into her anus. She backed her bottom up against him, eagerly awaiting the invasion of his cock. Grant pressed his cock head at her rear entrance, pausing for a brief moment before thrusting into her rectum to the hilt.

A sharp intake of breath caught in her throat. How could she have forgotten how wondrous it felt to experience the delicious sensation of being thoroughly stretched by two big cocks? Clinging to Rafe, she moved her bottom against Grant. "Please make love to me."

She didn't have to ask twice before they began to move together, timing their thrusts with synchronized choreography, pushing and driving into her holes, branding India their woman.

Clawing at Rafe's chest, she moaned her desire for them, unable to utter any words of coherence. She never wanted this moment to end, because it was together like this when everything made sense, when there were no doubts about their future and no one else's opinion mattered. The only thing that did was how she felt for them.

She wasn't sure how much time passed before she reached her climax. Neither Rafe nor Grant were finished with her, however. They continued to fuck her until she was once again caught up in a vortex of incendiary passion.

She tightened her pussy muscles around Rafe's cock, making him groan. "I'm coming," he said breathlessly. In the next instant, his seed shot into her thirsty sex.

Grant bit into her shoulder as he slammed into her bottom before shooting his load up her tight tunnel.

She reached another earth-shattering peak. It tore through her body like a tsunami, making her shake uncontrollably, until she went limp, completely spent.

None of them moved afterwards, content to remain in each other's arms. Drowsiness claimed her body. Her last thought before drifting off to sleep was how much she loved these two men, but was it enough?

Chapter Seventeen

India took a deep breath and squared her shoulders before ringing the doorbell of her parents' house. She felt like a child all over again, as her nerves threatened to get the better of her. Aunt Val had offered to come along with her even though Leila had made it clear her sister wouldn't be welcomed at this meal.

What was even harder was having said goodbye to her men earlier today. They'd spent the rest of the weekend in the hotel, making love and cuddling. When they were hungry, they ordered take out. Rafe and Grant took her body on a roller coaster of lust, passion and love.

Being with them had reaffirmed her feelings and made her realize she'd be happiest with them. India only had a few more loose ends to tie up concerning her affairs before she could move to Philadelphia, and it was decided that she make that journey within a month's time. They were all certain that by then no one would care who they were, and what was going on in their lives.

Still, there was one dark cloud hanging over their heads— Rafe's ex-wife. Both men were still adamant about giving in to that woman's demands, but India wasn't satisfied with that. While they were on the island, they had gone out of their way to protect her, and make sure she was safe. Now it was her chance to be their savior. The only problem was, she couldn't figure out how.

Saying goodbye to them had been hard, but she'd been brave, saving the tears until they had driven off. Once they were gone, a sense of doom filled her as she thought about the dinner party her mother was throwing.

India had taken extra care with her appearance even though she knew her mother would find some way to pick it apart. She'd armored herself with a new designer dress and matching pumps.

"Hello, little sis," Jack greeted when he answered the door. "You're looking...well." He always had a way of making a compliment sound like an insult.

They were never particularly close growing up. Jack had been too busy putting her down and making fun of her for any familial love to really develop between the two of then. There was a time when she worshipped the ground he walked on, he was her big brother after all, but Jack would have none of it. It was typical for older brothers to tease their little sisters, but taking his cue from her parents, his comments were with malicious intent to hurt.

"So do you," she returned without enthusiasm, knowing dinner was already going to be an ordeal, but with him there, it would be excruciating.

Jack remained where he stood, not bothering to let her past. "So, you're a celebrity of some sort aren't you?"

She shrugged. "I wouldn't say that. I'm sure as swiftly as the media latched on to the story, they'll forget it. Our story will be yesterday's news in no time. So are you going to open the door and let me in or do you plan on standing there staring at me?"

"Aren't you wondering why I'm here?" he demanded.

"Not particularly. You've always done what you've wanted, so I won't bother to guess your motives."

A smirk tilted his full lips. "That was a pretty impressive show you put on at your engagement party a few months ago. Poor Steven looked horrified. Mom said you made a mountain out of a molehill over something easily overlooked."

"I don't call finding him in bed with another woman a molehill."

A scowl crossed her brother's dark face. "What do you mean you caught him in bed with another woman? When did this happen? What are you talking about?"

Considering Jack never gave a damn about her, his sudden interest in what went down between her and Steven was surprising. "Since Mom seems to know it all, why don't you ask her? Now would you please let me in?"

He moved back just enough for her to squeeze inside, but when she would have gone further into the house, he grabbed her by the elbow.

"Tell me about this other woman? What did Steven say when you caught them together?"

"Why do you care? It's over and I don't intend on talking about it anymore." She pulled her arm from his grip and walked on.

Her mother was in the family room, setting out hors d'oeuvres on the coffee table. Leila lifted her head and smiled at India. "I'm glad you're here. You're just in time. I trust all is well with you?"

India searched for sarcasm in the comment and found none, then paused. Was her mother genuinely glad to see her or was she in the middle of some parallel universe where everything was the opposite of reality? First, her brother actually seemed like he cared about someone other than himself, and then her mother was being nice.

Not trusting what she'd heard, she cautiously replied, "I'm fine, thank you, Mom."

"You look nice, although I wish you wouldn't have had all your hair chopped off."

"Because it makes me look mannish?" India challenged, sure that was where her mother was heading.

"No. I wasn't going to say that, although longer hair *is* more feminine. Oh, well, it's only hair and it will grow back." Leila began fluffing the pillows on the couch. "Why don't you have a seat? Our guests should be here shortly, and your father will be down any minute now. He's upstairs shaving."

Apprehension filled India. Her mother was up to something and she wasn't sure she liked it. She felt like a fly being lured to the spider's web, and her mother was a big black widow, laying in wait for the kill.

"Who are your guests?" India asked, despite not knowing whether she wanted to hear the answer.

"Well, you remember Susan Mulligan, don't you? She's in our Jack and Jill chapter. I believe you used to have a crush on her son, didn't you? Anyway, her nephew is an editor at *The Washington Post*. She thought it would be a wonderful idea if the paper did an exposé on our family for the society column. Of course they wanted to highlight that little incident of yours, but I agreed it would be a fantastic idea."

She should have known. Her mother was only being nice, not because she'd had some change of heart, but because she wanted to parade India in front of some reporter and pretend they were a happy family. "By my little incident do you mean me being stuck on an island for two months?"

Her mother waved her hand dismissively. "Of course, India, why else would someone be interested in interviewing you?" There it was. India knew her mother couldn't go long without getting one little dig in.

"Why else indeed," she murmured. "But I'm not interested in being interviewed. I got enough of that when I was on Fuamatuu and I've already done the *Anne Webster Show*. I just wish people would leave me alone."

For a minute Leila's eyes narrowed, but then she hid her annoyance behind a carefully blank mask. "One more interview won't hurt. Besides, I plan on mentioning my garden club and the charity event we're throwing. And your father thinks it would be great to mention his business. A little promo can't hurt."

"And what's Jack going to plug?"

"Stop being silly. He's just here for moral support like a good brother should be. He's such a thoughtful boy," she sighed. "When I called him and told him about this interview he offered to come over. Naturally, I'll have to mention what a rising star he is at his job."

Jack was hardly that. He never stayed at a job longer than a few months. She was surprised he still had the same one as before she left for her vacation, but she decided to keep that comment to herself. India wanted no part of this whatsoever.

She stood up. "It seems like you three have this interview all planned out, so I don't see why I'm needed here. If I would have known, I would have passed. I'm not comfortable about this."

Her mother turned on her then, the mask off. "But you will stay for this interview. I've gone through a lot of trouble to arrange this and I won't have you messing it up, now sit down and be quiet and when the reporter asks you questions, smile and answer them appropriately."

"I'm sorry, but I can't. I want no part of this. You set this interview up, so you deal with the reporter."

Her father chose that moment to enter the living room. He gave India a brief nod of acknowledgement before noticing the tension in the room. "What's going on in here?"

Leila's plum smeared lips were pulled down into a deep frown. "Why don't you ask your daughter the ingrate?"

He turned his narrowed gaze in India's direction, but directed the question to his wife. "What's the girl done now?"

"She doesn't want to do the interview, after I practically had to kiss Susan's feet. You know I can't stand that woman. I can't believe I had to lower myself to ask her anything. And now your daughter is threatening to ruin it all."

Trevor folded his arms. "What's this nonsense your mother is talking about? Of course you're going to do this interview. Your mother went to a lot of trouble to set this up for you, and the least you can do is show your appreciation by answering a few questions. You owe us that much for raising you."

India's insides began to churn. The tension strumming within her body made her heartbeat speed up to an erratic pace. Who were they kidding? Her mother didn't set this interview up for her. They'd done it for themselves, to show off to their friends what a perfect family they were.

The doorbell rang before she could argue any further. Leila shot India one last stare before heading for the door. "You had better not ruin this for us, India."

Jack chose that moment to walk back into the room, and he flopped down on the sofa. "It looks like one of the special guests has arrived." He grabbed one of the cheese puffs and popped it into his mouth.

There was something in the way her brother said it that made India turn around to stare at him. "What are you talking about? Isn't it just the reporter?"

Again, that smirk she hated so much appeared on his lips. "Didn't Mom and Dad tell you the rest?" He looked at their father with an amused smile. "I guess you two were keeping the other part of this dinner a surprise. This will be interesting."

"Jack, please," Trevor lightly chided his son.

India didn't have to wait long to figure out what her parents were up to, when her ex walked in the door. Steven strode into the room like he owned it, his eyes locked on India's.

Her jaw dropped. Just when she thought this day couldn't possibly get worse it did.

ᙯ

Just as Grant drove across the Pennsylvania border, he realized he'd left something behind.

India.

"It's no use, Rafe." He finally broke the silence after being in the car for nearly three hours. Grant didn't bother to elaborate, knowing Rafe would understand exactly what he meant.

Letting India go yet again had been even harder than the first time. There was no way he could continue with this weekend arrangement even though it was only going to be for a month. Sure they'd agreed they give each other time to make the appropriate arrangements, but it wasn't soon enough. He needed her with them now.

"Yes. I couldn't stop thinking since we drove off. It worries me when we're away from her. She still has doubts about our arrangement and she might be susceptible to outside influences. I thought her aunt was a nice lady, but I got the feeling she didn't quite approve of us somehow."

"I thought I was imagining things, but I got that feeling too, especially when we went back to her house on Sunday morning for breakfast. She kept giving us funny looks," Grant recalled.

"Well, India did say her aunt knows about us. I'm sure Val knew what the three of us were up to this weekend. No, I don't think she'll be a problem. I get the feeling Val will support her niece in anything she decides to do. What I'm concerned about are India's parents. She told us she was having dinner with them tonight because they were throwing a dinner party. I get the sinking suspicion they may be up to something."

"That thought crossed my mind as well, or maybe they've experienced a change of heart where India is concerned."

Rafe laughed humorlessly. "Yeah, like our parents had a change of heart about us."

Grant shuddered as he thought of his last meeting with his dad. To exorcise some of his old demons he'd gone back to that old house and was surprised to see his father still living there. He looked twenty years older than what Grant knew his actual age to be, and he was just as drunk and belligerent as ever, but Grant was no longer a scared little boy. He was a man and could finally see what a sad, pathetic person the man who'd sired him actually was. He was weak, and because of that weakness, he tore others down to make himself feel better. A few years later Grant hadn't batted an eye when he learned of his father's death caused by a knife wound at a bar fight.

Rafe hadn't seen his mother in years, but the last he'd heard from her, she was living with yet another man.

"When put like that, I catch your meaning. I wonder what it

is they want with her? She hasn't had the time to heal from the pain they've inflicted on her over the years, as we have."

Rafe nodded. "Exactly. Imagine what being around them for any period of time would do to her self-esteem. I can't help but remember how starved of love she was when we first met her. It was as if she felt she wasn't worthy of anyone loving or caring about her. I believe it's one of the reasons she's always plagued with uncertainties when we're not there with her. Anyway, I don't think I can go another week without her here with us. I'd miss her too much.

"Are we in agreement about what we need to do?"

"Yes. Take the next exit and head back. I, for one, don't intend to leave without her this time around."

Chapter Eighteen

India's jaw dropped from lack of anything to say. Steven walked over to her, looking like the epitome of tall, dark and handsome. His chiseled ebony features and lithe, wide-shouldered body would have been enough to make any woman's pulse race, but she felt absolutely nothing. Not one single feeling stirred within her except disgust with herself for putting up with this joker for so long.

Steven leaned over and kissed her on the cheek. "You look very beautiful, India. I'm very glad I've had this opportunity to see you again. When I heard about the plane crash, I realized whatever silly difference we had doesn't matter. We belong together, and I'm willing to take you back, despite your little temper tantrum and embarrassing me in front of my friends and family. But I digress. We'll talk about this after the interview."

Trevor Powers beamed, holding his hand out to him. "It's so good of you to make it. When Leila told me you were coming, I was thrilled to hear you wouldn't hold what India did against her, and give her another chance. I can't think of anyone I'd rather have as a son-in-law than you."

India, still unable to believe what was going on, looked from her mother, whose smug expression said it all, to Steven's beaming face. The ringing doorbell prevented her from telling them both where to stuff it. This time it would probably be the reporter.

When India turned to look at her brother, she was nearly bowled over by the intensity of his glare. If there was ever any doubt in her mind about his feelings for her, there were none now. He hated her, but somehow it didn't cut as deeply as it used to.

Whatever Jack's problem was, she didn't have time to dwell on it because Steven wrapped his arm around her waist, giving the appearance of intimacy between them.

She would have pulled away from him, but his grip tightened. He leaned over to whisper in her ear, "There's no need to be so squeamish, India. We'll talk about your little outburst later. Now smile for the reporter."

A petite brunette with warm brown eyes walked forward and held her hand out to India. "Miss Powers, it's a pleasure to finally meet you. When I heard about your brave tale, I was honored to be chosen to be the one to tell your story. I'm Ellen Finster, but please call me Ellen."

India could only stare at the woman until Steven gave her a light pinch, jolting her into action. She took the offered hand and tried to shape her lips into a smile. It wasn't this woman's fault that her parents had manipulated India into this situation. "Nice to meet you and you may call me India."

"That's such a pretty name." There was something genuine about the other woman that India would have found warming under any other circumstances, but with her family and Steven hovering around, she couldn't bring herself to relax.

"Thank you," India muttered.

Ellen's smile widened and she flashed large white news-anchor teeth. "No, thank *you* for granting me this interview. I've been doing so many hard-hitting exposés lately, a human interest story is something I could really sink my teeth into, and people are still very much enthralled by your experiences. We were so surprised because other than your appearance on the *Anne Webster Show*, you and your fellow survivors have stayed out of the public eye. But I can understand you'd want to get back into some form of normalcy."

India could have laughed at that one. With Rafe and Grant, her life would never be normal again.

Her mother was all smiles. "And of course we're all so glad to have India back with us. You might be familiar with her fiancé, Steven Cartwright. His father used to be a congressman for several years and now heads the prestigious Cartwright law firm. Steven just might be following his father's footsteps and throw his hat in the political ring. We're sure he'll be successful in any endeavor," Leila gushed.

Ellen wore a slight smile, not giving anything away from her expression. "I'm sure he will. So, India, how would you like this interview to go? Would you like to sit out here, or would you prefer some privacy to chat."

The expression on her mother's face said it all. She hadn't expected this turn of events. "It's my understanding this was to be a family interview," she sputtered.

"Of course, I wanted to see India in her home environment interacting with her family, if you will, but she will be the focus. However I do plan on asking a few questions about how the plane's disappearance affected you and how you felt when you learned India had been found."

Leila couldn't hide her chagrin fast enough. She'd gone through so much trouble setting everything up as if they would all be the stars when the truth was, India would steal all the glory—attention India could do without.

Trevor stepped forward, seeming no more pleased than his wife. "If you'd like to get the family's interaction, then the best way for you to do so is to have dinner with us. We'd be pleased for you to join us and I'm sure India wouldn't mind your interviewing her at the table. We have no secrets from each other."

Ellen shot India a questioning look. "Would that be okay with you, India?"

"She won't mind," Steven answered for her.

Ellen ignored him. "India?"

"I..." She looked from her mother to her father, and they both gave her thunderous looks, daring her to contradict them or make a scene. As much as she wanted to walk out the door and never come back, something within her crumbled. How was it that they had the ability to do this to her firm resolve each and every time? Besides, causing a scene would have embarrassed Ellen as much as it would her family and Steven. "No, I don't mind."

The smile returned to her mother's lips. "Dinner is served. We're having lamb shank with a rosemary mint sauce. I hope that's alright, Ellen."

The reporter nodded. "That sounds lovely. Thank you."

Her mother took Ellen by the arm and began telling her about her next charity shindig. When Steven would have led India to the dining room, she managed to break away from him. After experiencing something so beautiful and magical with Rafe and Grant, having his hands on her made India's skin crawl.

"What's your problem?" he whispered in her ear. "Your mother said you'd be glad to see me. You'd better start acting like it, girl, or I will walk out of here right now. I can have any woman I want, you know."

She wanted to ask why he wasn't with one of them, if that was the case, but Jack was suddenly right behind them.

"Do I detect a little trouble in paradise?" There was a light taunt to Jack's tone.

Steven barely spared her brother a glance. "Everything is fine, Jackson, not that it's any of your concern?"

Jack's voice lowered a decibel although India heard him loud and clear. "Why do you insist on being so formal with me? You've never had any problem calling me Jack before...or Jackie baby."

Steven turned around and shot him a look of pure venom. "You had better keep your damn mouth shut, Jackson, if you know what's good for you."

India could remain silent no longer. Something was definitely going on here. "I don't know what you two are arguing about, and frankly, I don't care," she said tight-lipped, "but you'd better save it for another time. I'm not in the mood to hear it."

Jack's eyes narrowed. "Considering this affects you, dear little sister, you ought to care."

Steven looked as if he wanted to punch her brother in the mouth, and India wasn't sure if he would have or not, when the three of them were called to the table.

"Jack, Steven and India, dinner is ready," she called out. The gaiety in her mother's tone sounded false to India's ears.

Her mother motioned India to the foot of the table, the chair usually reserved for Leila. "Since you're the guest of honor, you should sit here." India knew what her mother was up to the minute she took the seat next to Ellen while the next closest occupant sitting at the head of the table was her father. Steven didn't look happy when Jack took the seat next to him.

Thus began one of the most excruciating meals she'd ever suffered through. Every time Ellen asked a question, her mother would interrupt and answer for her. What got to India was the hypocrisy.

Her parents pretended they'd been devastated when they learned of the plane's disappearance. At one point the frustrated reporter gave up, but it didn't stop Leila from talking.

Ellen tried to direct the focus back to India with steely determination. "So, *India*." She emphasized the name, making it clear to all whom the question was directed to. "Could you tell me a little about your experience on the island and how you felt when you learned you were one of three survivors?"

India put the fork down she'd been using to toy with her food. "I was scared," she answered honestly. "There were four of us who actually survived the plane crash, but one of us obviously didn't last that first night. We buried him and that's when it hit home that we were on our own. I can't pretty up my experience and say we lived some *Gilligan's Island* type fantasy, it was grittier, more harrowing, not knowing where our next meal would come from...or whether someone would come rescue us. Those first couple days were the hardest, but we somehow managed to get by. If it weren't for Rafe and Grant, I doubt I would have made it."

When she thought of them, a smile touched her lips. She'd only seen them a few hours ago, but she felt like a part of her was missing. More than anything she wished she could go be with them.

Leila smiled indulgently. "And we're so proud of her, aren't we Trevor?"

Her father merely grunted.

To finally hear those words from her mother's lips was like a double-edged sword. She'd been waiting all her life to hear them, but they held no meaning because there was no truth behind it. India knew her parents could have cared less whether she'd lived or died.

Suddenly, everything she'd been holding in finally burst forward. "Are you really, Mom? Proud of me, I mean?"

Leila's composure slipped for a moment, but the careful smile she'd pasted on her lips remained. "Of course I am, dear, I'm your mother. I'm proud of both of my children. Our Jackson is a rising star at the accounting firm he works at. Why don't you tell her a little about it, honey. I'm sure India is tired of being the center of attention."

"Because heaven forbid, I get any attention at all, right?" India didn't care how it might have looked to Ellen, who was now squirming in her chair with a look of distinct discomfort.

Trevor gave India a quailing look. "India! That's enough. Now isn't the time to play the diva." Her father must have realized how that might have sounded to the reporter, and tried to soften his words with a smile, but the damage was already done. He turned to his son. "Jack, tell the lady about your job," Trevor said gruffly trying to switch the conversation away from his outburst.

Jack had spent the entire meal sending her and Steven resentful stares. "I no longer work there," he finally answered. "I'm currently looking for something else," he muttered, stabbing a piece of lamb with his fork before stuffing a hearty bite in his mouth.

The shock was evident on her parents' faces. Once again the apple of their eye had pulled a stunt which India would have received a scathing tongue-lashing for.

"You never said anything, Jack," her mother scolded lightly. "Although I'm sure you had a good reason. You're a go-getter. Not willing to settle for something mediocre. You'll find something in no time I'm sure."

"Mother, would you just shut up!" Jack's sudden outburst surprised them all.

Leila gasped in surprise. India had seen Jack talk to their parents any way he pleased in the past, but she never would have imagined he'd do it in front of witnesses. The hurt look on her mother's face didn't move India a bit. A stunned silence fell across the room, no one moving.

Ellen pushed away from the table. "I'm sorry, but I'll have to continue this interview another time when there aren't so many distractions. Don't worry, I'll see myself out." She walked over to India. "I'm sorry we didn't get a chance to talk properly, but please, give me a call when you're ready. I would love to chat with you one-on-one." She produced a small rectangular business card from her breast pocket and handed it to India. "This has my work, home and cell phone numbers. Give me a call when you're ready."

And with that, the reporter got the hell out of Dodge. Instead of directing their anger to her brother where it belonged, her parents turned the force of their glares to her. "India, join us in the living room. We'd like to have a word with you," her father began tightly, obviously not wanting to have any further outbursts in front of Steven, who'd remained oddly silent for the duration of the meal.

India removed the napkin from her lap and stood, finally coming to the epiphany that she was wasting her time by being here, and attempting to have a relationship with them. Hadn't they told her in so many ways already that she wasn't loved and they could never love her? Knowing there were two men out there who loved her unconditionally, neurosis and all, gave India the strength she needed now. "No. I won't. Why should I? After all, Steven's going to be family, isn't he?"

Steven looked distinctly uncomfortable. "Look, I should go also."

India turned to him. "No. Stay where you are. You were quite eager to show up when you heard a reporter was going to be here to interview me. Did you think I'd bring you some much needed publicity? You have the most gigantic ego I've ever known anyone to have. Did you think just because my mother called you, I would come running back to you? Newsflash: you're not God's gift and I certainly have no intention of ever getting back together with you. Did you think I would after I saw you in bed with some other woman?"

Her father slammed his fist against the table. "That's enough? Haven't you embarrassed us enough today already?"

"Please, Steven, she doesn't know what she's saying," Leila pleaded, seeing her aspirations of a politician's mother-in-law slip away. "Explain to her that other woman was just a silly misunderstanding."

"Yes, explain to us," Jack demanded. "I'd especially like to know considering—"

Steven stood up abruptly. "I don't have to listen to any of this. I'm sorry I got mixed up with this crazy family."

Jack halted, grabbing his arm. "Sorry you got mixed up with us, because you realized you couldn't have the brother and the sister too?"

A collective gasp filled the room. India only had to look at the expressions on Steven's and Jack's faces to know what her brother said was true. It suddenly made sense why there seemed to be so much tension between the two men, and why Steven seemed more hostile to her than usual. Not only that, it suddenly occurred to India that at one time her brother and ex-fiancé had been on pretty friendly terms, but had something come between them to change that? The other woman she'd seen Steven with, perhaps?"

Steven turned a deep shade of purple. "Take your goddamn hands off of me, you goddamn queer."

Jack chuckled. "If I'm queer, what does that make you? Should I tell everyone in the room how you'd beg for it? What if I let it be known that you had planned on marrying my sister, and carrying on your affair with me? How you couldn't wait for me to screw you? Or, and this is a good one," Jack laughed, "before we became lovers, you had a thing for trannies?" A malicious smile curved Jack's lips. "I'm wondering if it was a woman India saw you with at all and not one of your other little friends. Is that why you cut me off so abruptly? Because you found a new playmate? Who was she? Or should I say he?"

India's eyes widened. Though she hadn't gotten a good look at the woman's face, there had been something a bit masculine about her. India wanted to throw up when she realized how thoroughly close she'd come to being duped. They would have gotten married and he would have continued to carry on affairs—and possibly with her own brother."

"I don't have to listen to this," Steven mumbled indignantly, hauling his arm out of Jack's grip.

"That's fine, I already got what I wanted from you anyway, and you enjoyed giving it to me." Jack turned to India then. "He was using you, little sis, because you were the perfect trophy wife who probably wouldn't demand too much of his time while he was out playing. I bet he even thought you might have guessed where his preferences lay and tried to reconcile with you so you would keep your mouth shut."

Jack must have hit the nail on the head because the next thing she knew, Steven slammed his fist into Jack's mouth. "You shut your filthy mouth, you fucking fa—"

"Don't!" India interrupted. There had already been too

much ugliness spouted in this room already. She couldn't stand to hear another word of it. "Just go, Steven."

Steven looked like he wanted to administer another blow to Jack, who was laid out on the floor, nursing a busted lip, chuckling at the havoc he'd wreaked.

"India, he's lying." Steven gave her an imploring look.

She shook her head. "Somehow I doubt that."

With a muttered curse under his breath, Steven stormed out the room, not bothering to look back.

India looked at her parents, who seemed to have had the wind knocked out of them. She already knew their views on homosexuality. They thought it was disgusting, and they had never bitten their tongues about it either. Finding out their favorite child was one of "those" probably devastated them. Yet India didn't feel a bit of pity for them.

She walked over to Jack to see if he was okay. "Jack, how's your lip?"

"I got a punch in the mouth, what do you think?" he sneered. "Now the secret is out, do you want to gloat?"

She'd felt many things for her brother at one point in her life or other, love, hero-worship, anger and jealousy. India never believed one of those emotions would be pity.

"You know I was jealous of you?" he said quietly.

She was surprised to hear him say it. "Of me? But you were always the one with the attention, and you got everything you wanted."

"And I hated it. I saw you trying so hard to gain their acceptance even though I knew you never would, but you've accomplished so much. Me on the other hand, I screwed up so many times, sometimes on purpose but they still put me on that pedestal. Even though you never saw it, you were so together, and I wasn't. I couldn't quite get a handle on things in my life. I didn't want to be worshipped for the son they thought I was. I wanted to be loved for who I was. I know I haven't treated you so well, but I was jealous as hell of you, and for that, I'm sorry."

"I didn't realize."

"You couldn't have. I just wanted to say, I bear you no ill will."

All the years of animosity she'd felt for him melted away in that moment. She couldn't hate him anymore. She wasn't sure if she ever did. Jack was just as much a victim of Leila and Trevor's crummy parenting skills as she was. For the first time in her life, she finally felt like she could have a relationship with her brother.

"This probably wasn't the ideal way to come out, but maybe now you can be happy?"

A slight grin touched his swollen lips and then he grimaced in pain. "You know. I think I just might. Thanks, little sis. You're not so bad after all."

She held her hand out to him, providing Jack leverage to get off the floor. She'd forgotten her parents' presence in the room.

"Look, I need to get out of here, now. There's someplace I need to be. If you ever need to...to talk, Aunt Val will always have my current numbers."

He nodded.

She didn't know whether to hug him goodbye or not. After all, it was difficult to change a twenty-nine-year habit. Compelled to cement their newfound understanding, she stood on the tip of her toes and brushed her lips against his cheek. "Take care."

Without sparing her parents another look, she headed out of the dining room. She was almost to the door when she heard footsteps behind her. India was grabbed and turned around to meet the angry gaze of her mother. "This is all your fault! I know it is!" Leila screamed frantically. "I wished you'd died in that plane crash! Why did you have to come back and mess up everything?" There was a crazed look on the older woman's face.

A long time ago, perhaps even a few months prior, that comment would have killed her inside, but it barely put a dent in her soul. Her parents no longer had the power to hurt her. She'd found the strength she never thought she had, and realized, she didn't need them in her life. As a matter of fact, she would do better than fine without them.

For a long time India wondered what she would say to either one of her parents if she ever had the courage to say what she wanted to them. Now she did. She smiled at her mother. "You know what, Leila? I don't give a shit what you think. Have a nice life." And with that she turned on her heel and walked out of her parents' home for the last time, knowing she would never be back.

Finally her demons had been set free. And now there was only one thing left, and that was to reunite with her men.

Chapter Nineteen

When Grant pulled his car into Val's driveway, Rafe noted India's car was missing. If she was still at dinner with her parents, he had every intention of getting their address and going to get her.

Without waiting for Grant to shut off the engine, Rafe tore the door open and shot out of his seat. He made it to the door and rang the doorbell before Grant caught up with him.

Grant chuckled. "You could have waited until I stopped the car at least."

"Had I been driving, you probably would have done the same thing." He rang the doorbell again, in his impatience.

"Probably."

Rafe tapped his foot. Where was that woman and why wasn't she answering the door. He was about to ring the bell again when Val opened the door.

"Rafe! Grant! I'm glad it's you and not a solicitor because I was about to curse you out for ringing my doorbell like that. What are you doing here?"

"We've come to get India. Is she still at her parent's house?" Rafe demanded.

"I would imagine. I haven't heard from her since she left a few hours ago. Why don't you come in and wait for her." She stepped back, opening the door wide.

"If it's all the same to you, would you mind providing the address to her parents' house and we'll meet her there."

Val raised a brow. "I don't see any point in giving you the address when she should be back any minute now. Anyway, I'm glad you guys came back, because I wanted to talk to you both."

Rafe wanted to argue, but thought better of it, besides, he didn't think there was any use. Petite she might be, Val was a formidable woman. With a sigh, he went inside.

"Have a seat, you two. I'll get you something to drink? What will it be?"

"Nothing for me, thank you," Grant said sitting down on the couch.

"Rafe?"

"Coke would be fine, thanks."

He fidgeted in his seat until she returned with his soda. "Thank you."

She took the chair opposite of them. "How was your drive?"

"It was fine." Grant asked cautiously, "Do you have any idea what time India should be back?"

"Like I said, I don't think she'll be much longer. Relax, she'll be back soon enough. I can't imagine why she'd linger. To be honest, I was a bit worried about her going over there on her own. I'd offered to go with her, but she insisted I didn't. I'm not sure how much you know about the situation with her parents, but it always concerns me when she's with them for any amount of time."

Rafe took a sip of his cola before answering. "She's told us quite a bit, and we share your concerns. Val, can I be frank with you?"

"Certainly, if you allow me the same courtesy."

Rafe placed his drink on the coffee table. "We're aware that India has told you what happened between the three of us on the island, and I want you to know it wasn't just a sex thing—if that's what you're thinking. It was special, and though it might not be a conventional arrangement, we love her and she loves us. So if you wanted to try to talk us out of taking her with us, I believe you'd be wasting your time."

"I see," she murmured. "It wasn't my intention to talk you out of anything. India's a grown woman and she can do as she pleases. My concern is that she doesn't get hurt. She's told you about her parents so you know she's already suffered enough. My niece is very special to me, and for my peace of mind, I'd like to be assured this isn't some perverted experiment you two are conducting."

Grant raised his brows. "I'm sorry, but I resent that 'perverted' remark. Why is it perverted? Because the two of us love her and are willing to share? That rather than letting a woman come between the bond Rafe and I have, we've decided to choose one woman we can both love? Why is it perverted if it's a tender, loving relationship? It's not monogamous for her, but it would be for us. Besides that, instead of one man to take care of and love her as she deserves, she'll have the both of us. I'm not saying everything will be smooth sailing—no relationship is, but neither one of us would ever do anything to hurt her. So no, this isn't some experiment to us. It's ours lives—she's our lives."

Val didn't answer immediately, giving them one long look. She rubbed her chin and examined them intently before she finally replied. "I believe you. And I believe you believe what you're saying. I wouldn't be having this conversation if I didn't like the two of you and it's quite obvious that you're both quite taken with India. But I guess what I'm trying to understand is how two good-looking, virile men like yourselves chose this lifestyle."

Rafe knew he'd have to give her the entire story in order for her to understand the big picture. With a sigh, he started from the beginning, from the time they were children up until Rafe's marriage and then when they met India. By the time he was finished, there were tears in Val's eyes.

"Oh, you poor babies! I'm so sorry you two had to go through that. Some people shouldn't be parents. I thought my sister and brother-in-law took the lousy parents award, but they might be tied with yours. It all makes sense why the three of you gravitated toward each other the way you did. Perhaps you recognized in each other a mutual pain that could only be healed by someone who understood true suffering. My niece has unfortunately suffered, as have the two of you."

Rafe nodded. He hadn't thought of it like that before. He supposed she was right. "Something like that. Listen, Val, we only have the intention of making her happy, and you have my word on that. I would rather cut my heart out than hurt her."

"I second that. She means a lot to me as well, and I know it's reciprocated."

"India loves the two of you also. She's been moping around the house since she's been back, pining for you. Your lifestyle may not be easily accepted by others, so you may have some rough patches ahead because of narrow-minded people, but I wish you all the best. And let me tell you right now. If you do hurt my niece, you'll have to answer to me. I may be small, but I'll kick your asses."

Rafe and Grant burst into simultaneous laugher.

The three of them were getting along like old friends, when Rafe heard the lock of the front door turning. He stood, knowing it was India and his heart began to beat faster. Even though he'd seen her earlier today, it seemed like a long time.

Grant's face mirrored his anticipation.

India walked into the living room looking absolutely gorgeous. "I thought I saw your car outside, but I didn't want to believe... I'm—"

Rafe held his arms open wide to her and she flung herself into them, bursting into sobs. Even a few hours was too much time to be away from the men she loved. She showered his face with kisses. "I missed you so much. So, so much." India pulled away from him to give Grant the same treatment, pressing her lips over his laughing face.

Rafe moved behind her, pressing his body against her back. "We missed you too much, baby."

Val coughed loudly, making her presence known. "Ahem, I'm standing here."

India laughed. "I'm sorry, I was just so happy to see them."

"But you just saw them today. Sheesh. Should I give you crazy kids some time alone?" Val rolled her eyes.

Rafe placed a kiss on the side of India's neck. "That won't be necessary. We only plan on staying long enough for India to pack so we can take her with us." He gently turned India around to face him and pressed his lips against her in a swift, hard kiss. "And I don't want any arguments out of you. You're coming with us, and that's that."

She grinned "And what will you do if I don't want to."

His eyes narrowed. "I hope you're joking because if you aren't, I'm going to throw you over my shoulder and walk out of this house with you!"

India turned her head to look at Grant with a playful pout. "Would you let this big meanie do that to me?"

Grant nodded without hesitation. "Absolutely. I'd be right there behind him, giving your luscious backside a much needed smack for trying to thwart us."

"Well, when put like that, I guess I'll have to come with you then, but lucky for you, I had already planned on driving to Philly tonight."

"You never mentioned this to me before you went to your parents' house? When did you make that decision?" Val asked.

India pulled out of their holds. "Take a seat because you simply won't believe this."

Val sighed. "Nothing my sister does ceases to amaze me. What did she do this time?"

Once the four of them had taken a seat with Rafe and Grant on either side of India on the couch. She began her story, telling them of how she'd been tricked by her mother, who'd set up an interview with *The Post*. Rafe was glad he'd never met the Powers because he wanted to throttle both of them.

When India got to the part about Jack's outburst, Val exclaimed, "Get outta here. You've got to be joking."

India held up her right hand. "I swear to God. He outted himself and Steven. It suddenly makes sense why Steven wanted us to wait for sex until after we were married. I'm not saying that's a bad thing, but it always made me wonder why, because he didn't strike me as the celibate type. Even when we were kissing, something seemed to be a bit off. Now I know he wasn't interested in women, or maybe it was just me. Anyway, Steven was so angry, he called Jack a derogatory name, and then punched him square in the mouth."

Val covered her mouth with her hand. "Oh my God. Your mother probably had a fit."

"Actually, she and Trevor sat in stunned silence, as Jack and I kind of had a little reconciliation believe it or not. But don't worry. Leila stayed true to form. Just before I walked out the door, she said something that was meant to hurt me, but it only made me a little sad."

Rafe kissed her on the cheek. "Why did it make you sad, India?"

"Sad for all the years I've wasted trying to live up to an ideal that never existed. And sad for not realizing sooner that the only person that was making me unhappy was me. I let them do that to me. But in a way, I'm glad this happened because now I'm going to take that happiness that I've been denied for so long for myself. And I know I'd be happiest with you and Grant. When we came back from the island, I was so scared and worried about what other people would say about us, not focusing on that special bond we shared, but I'm tired of living like that. I want to be happy with you two." She took Grant's and Rafe's hands in each of hers and gave them a nice squeeze."

"If I might make a suggestion," Val interrupted, "I think the three of you should spend the night and drive back in the morning. It's getting dark out there. Besides, it doesn't sound like you had much dinner at your parents' house. I'll fix you something to eat."

"Just a couple hot dogs will be fine with me," India answered.

Rafe leaned over and whispered in her ear, a smile tugging the corners of his lips. "I have a hot dog for you."

India smacked him on the knee with a giggle. "Don't get fresh when you're not in the position to do anything about it."

Rafe whispered again. "Name it and I'll get into any position you want."

She shook her head with mock exasperation. "What am I going to do with you, Rafe?"

"Love me."

"I already do. Very much."

Long after her aunt had gone to bed, the three lovers sat on the couch, talking and cuddling. India had never felt so content in her life and all it had taken was for her to just let go.

She sat between Grant's thighs as he massaged her shoulders while her feet rested on Rafe's legs.

"Mmm. Grant, that feels lovely. Don't stop."

"If I don't, my hands won't be the only thing rubbing you." Grant kneaded her flesh.

"You two are so nasty."

"But you wouldn't have us any other way." Rafe's lips tilted in a wicked grin.

"What time do you think we'll be heading out tomorrow? There's something I need to do," she finished with a yawn, lethargy starting to take over.

"I was thinking we should venture out after rush hour traffic. There's no way I'm going to miss out on your aunt's chocolate chip pancakes," Grant answered. "What was it you had to do?"

"I'm going to put an end to Angie's blackmail plans once and for all."

Rafe sat up straight from his relaxed position. "What are you talking about?"

"Like I said before, I'm not going to allow you guys to give in to her demands and it's not even the money. It's the principle. She doesn't deserve a dime, and she certainly shouldn't get it by extortion. If my plan works, she won't have a leg to stand on."

Rafe frowned. "What do you plan on doing?"

"Remember I was telling you about that reporter who was at the dinner?"

"No!" Grant protested.

"Yes. This is the only way. If we beat Angie to the punch there will be no story to tell, hence no blackmail."

"India, do you know what could possibly happen if you tell this reporter about our relationship. It may bring you some unwanted attention. That's what we want to shield you from."

"But that's just it. You don't have to protect me. If the world knows about us, I don't care. I know I'm strong enough to deal with it."

"But in your profession, some people may take issue with it," Rafe pointed out.

"Then if it comes to that, we'll deal with it, but my mind is made up and I'm going to do this interview. It's my turn to look out for the two of you."

Rafe's shoulders drooped in defeat. He probably realized it was pointless to argue with her. "You don't have to do this."

"I know I don't, but I want to. And I'm going to. If we're to start our lives together, I want it to be with a clean slate, with no shadows from the past. No pains or regrets and certainly no ex-wives popping up."

Grant wrapped his arms around her waist, and she leaned back into his warmth. Rafe crawled toward her and planted a kiss on her lips. "You're an amazing woman, do you know that?"

"Wait until tomorrow night, and I'll show you just how

amazing I can be." She giggled. "You two aren't the only ones who have your minds in the gutter."

Chapter Twenty

Ellen showed up at nine o'clock on the dot as she'd promised. India felt bad for calling her so late at night, but the other woman didn't seem to mind. She'd actually sounded quite pleased.

"Thank you so much for coming here on such short notice," India greeted her when she answered the door.

The reporter gave her a genuine smile. "No, don't worry about it. And believe me the pleasure is all mine. I really didn't think I'd hear from you again, so when you called me, to say not only would you do the interview, but you had the other two survivors with you as well, I was in hog heaven. Stories like these don't come along often and I'm glad you thought of me when you decided to share yours."

"Please come in. Have you had breakfast? There's plenty leftover. We have chocolate chip pancakes as well as blueberry ones, turkey bacon, grit and eggs."

Ellen shook her head. "Mmm, that sounds delicious, but I'm trying to watch my weight. My high school reunion is coming up and I'm trying to slim down so I can get into this Calvin Klein dress I bought at a killer sale. I had to have it when I saw it, but unfortunately it was a size too small." She patted her stomach with regret.

"Can I at least get you a cup of coffee?"

"That sounds wonderful. Black with two teaspoons of sugar, please."

"Coming right up, and the men are in the living room so you can go ahead and introduce yourselves to each other."

India wished her aunt could have been here for the interview as well. After all, she was India's closest family member. Aunt Val was a free lance editor who did a lot of her work from home, but occasionally she had to go into the office. This morning happened to be one of those times, but her aunt promised to be back in time to see the three of them off.

Her aunt had been more of a mother to her than Leila Powers could ever be. India could no longer think of those two people who'd sired her as her parents. Real parents would have loved her unconditionally and wouldn't have gone out of their way to make her life miserable. For so long, India had wished she knew what it was about them that had made them treat her the way they did, or if there was something wrong with her. Now, none of it mattered. They were out of her life for good.

On a bright note, maybe she and Jack could finally forge that brother and sister bond they'd never had. She much preferred to be his friend than his enemy. Maybe now that he was out of the closet, he could find someone to love without being secretive about it. She credited her brother for her decision to have this interview. All his life, he'd been miserable, obviously ashamed of who he was. India realized she didn't want to live like that.

India returned to the living room with coffee mug in hand, and offered it to Ellen.

"Thank you so much. I was running a bit late this morning so I didn't get a chance to stop for a cup."

India took a seat in between her men on the couch. "This beats the stuff in the convenient stores. My aunt brews it fresh."

Ellen took a sip. "Mmm. You're right." She placed the cup on the coffee table. "Now that everyone is here, shall we start?"

India took Rafe's and Grant's hands, unashamed of showing them affection in front of others. She could tell it didn't go unnoted by the other woman, who shot them a curious glance.

"India, if you would like for me to include a few quotes from your family in this article, I would be more than happy to," the reporter began.

"Rafe and Grant are my family, and my Aunt Val of course."

Ellen raised a dark brow. "I can infer from your comment the three of you became close on the island. Would you say it happened because you did what was necessary to survive?"

India looked from Rafe's smoldering Latin handsomeness to Grant's rugged All-American features, not bothering to hide what she felt for them before turning her attention back to Ellen. "We did have to depend on each other to survive, but it was much more than that, you see, the three of us fell in love. They with me and I with them."

Ellen shot the three of them a look of disbelief. "Is this something you want included in the interview?"

India waited to get silent consent from the men before answering for all three of them. "Yes. You see, none of us are ashamed of our feelings. The world may look on at us as an unconventional trio, but something special happened to us on the island. Yes, it was a daily struggle with fighting the elements, and wondering if we'd be rescued. We experienced things you wouldn't find in any movie or book and we went to bed hungry more times than I care to remember, but we managed because we had each other."

"But do you think your feelings stem from having been on

the island with no one to depend on except each other? They say in times of stress, people come together who may not in ordinary circumstances."

"We understand a lot of people will come to that conclusion, but I know this would have happened between the three of us regardless of the plane crash. Even at the airport, the attraction we shared was strong. Grant and I had already decided India was the woman of our dreams when we first laid eyes on her." Rafe patted India on the knee.

Ellen looked flustered for a moment, but then regained her composure. "So you two have done this before? Shared a woman?"

Grant nodded. "By accident, we discovered it was something we liked to do."

The reporter shook her head. "I'm sorry, but it's not likely I'll be able to put any of this in the paper. My editor would probably say I was making it up."

"You have your tape recorder," India pointed out.

"I know, but my point is, your story is more provocative than the types of stories *The Post* prints. Maybe we could focus more on your survival efforts."

"Would it be too provocative if it were just me and one man on the island?" India wanted to know.

"To be honest, no. I would probably be able to get away with writing about a great love story. But if people read this, we'd get complaints for sure." Ellen shook her head. "No. I'm sorry. I truly believe the three of you do share a special bond, but I can't do the story as you want me to."

India bit her bottom lip. If it didn't get printed, Angie could go to any rag she wanted. "It could still be a great love story, and I think you're just the reporter to do it."

"But—"

India held up her hand to halt the other woman's protest. "Just hear me out and if by the end of my story, you haven't changed your mind, then I'll respect your wishes."

Ellen looked like she wanted to argue, but then nodded. "Okay, but I make no promises."

"I understand." India told their tales, leaving nothing out, except the more graphic and intimate details of the story. She even told Ellen of Rafe's marriage and how his wife was trying to use their past to get more money from him and Grant. Then she finished her tale of how she finally gained strength through her love for these two men.

By the time India was finished, tears streamed down the reporter's face. India grabbed the box of tissues on the end table and handed it to the other woman.

"That was absolutely beautiful. I was skeptical when you made your surprise announcement, but now I understand. I do want to write this story, and I'll fight to get it printed, thank you so much for sharing it with me."

India grinned in triumph. Once that story hit the paper, Angie would have no tale to tell, because it would already be told.

Game. Set. Match.

It was later that afternoon when they pulled up to Grant's house. They'd decided they'd all live here until they found a bigger place together. Personally, India didn't care if they lived in a cardboard box, as long as she was with them. She didn't think it was possible to be in love with anyone as much as she was with them.

"So what do you think of your temporary new home?" Grant asked when they stepped inside.

"It's nice, although it definitely needs a woman's touch."

Rafe laughed, putting her suitcases down. "She's only been here for a few seconds and already she wants to redecorate. Women."

"Hey! I resemble that remark. Besides, there's really no point in redecorating if we're going to sell anyway, but I do insist I get a pink bathroom in our new home."

Grant groaned. "That's a sacred room for a man. Any color but pink."

"We'll compromise. Maybe peach for the bathroom and pink for the bedroom." She had no intention of turning their home into the Barbie Dream House, but India liked to tease them.

Rafe rolled his eyes heavenward. "I think we've created a monster, Grant."

Now that they were finally alone together, there was only one thing she wanted to do. "So are we all just going to stand around and talk or will you show me to the bedroom?"

"I thought you'd never asked." Grant scooped her into his arms.

"Put me down," she protested with a laugh.

"Not before we get to the bedroom," he countered.

Just as he promised he would, Grant carried her to his bedroom upstairs with Rafe right behind them, not setting India on her feet until they were on the side of the bed.

"I want to undress you both." She began to work on Grant's button-up shirt and slowly pushed it off his shoulders, then worked on his pants. Only when he stood magnificently naked before her, cock jutting forward in its hardness did she undress

Rafe with frantic movements.

Their hands were on her, disposing of India's clothing with the same frenzy she'd just displayed. When she stood nude and unashamed before them, Rafe lifted her and placed her in the middle of the bed.

She giggled, reveling in his strength. "What's the deal with you two lifting me up all the time?"

"It gives us the excuse to touch you, baby." Rafe grinned at her, his hands roaming her body.

Grant touched his lips to the beating pulse of her throat.

An exultant hunger like nothing she'd ever experienced soared through her body. India wanted to touch and caress them as well. Turning to her side to face Grant, she ran her fingers along his hard torso, circling his nipple with her finger tip. And then she leaned forward and repeated the motion with her tongue. The flat disk peaked in her mouth.

"Oh God, India." Grant groaned.

India allowed her hand to drift to his cock. She grasped it and gave it a gentle touch, making his body jerk in reaction.

He closed his eyes. "You don't know what you're doing to me," he muttered.

She had an idea.

Rafe ran his tongue along her back, to the base of her spine, sending pulses of heat coursing through her body.

India cried out when Rafe pushed her legs apart to bury his face in her pussy from behind. She pushed back, grinding her pussy into his face. Rafe stroked her sex with his tongue.

She couldn't get enough of them as they caressed, licked, stroked and did things to her body she'd only dreamt of before. There was only one thing she needed to make this moment just right and that was to have them inside of her. Unable to take the delicious torture any longer, India begged them to make love to her. "Please. I need it now. I want it right now!"

Rafe rolled away from her and slid off the bed while Grant rolled on his back and pulled her on top of him, positioning his cock against her moist slit.

She parted her folds, readying herself for him. India lowered her pussy over his dick, gasping as it stretched her walls, driving deep into her. "Mmm," she sighed her content and then waited for Rafe, who returned moments later with a small tube.

India bit her bottom lip as he rubbed the lubricant on his cock and then over her anus. She shivered with her eagerness to be with him.

Rafe parted her cheeks and slowly eased into her quivering ass. "Oh, Yeah."

Nothing could compare to this feeling of being with their cocks. Her love for these two gorgeous men only intensified the sensations coursing through her body.

"Make love to me," she whispered, unable to take the stillness any longer.

Grant grasped India by the waist and lifted her hips to thrust into her. Rafe slowly began to grind his cock inside her body.

It took them a few moments to catch their rhythm, but when they did, a frisson of hardcore delight spiraled through her body and exploded. She bucked her hips, accepting and squeezing their cocks within her orifices, loving every moment of the fire burning deep within her being. India couldn't get enough of the way their dicks stuffed her so deliciously. As they moved, each man whispered words of love to her and she murmured them back.

In this position, Grant's cock rubbed her clit, creating the most decadent sensation. She could barely stand it.

Tension coiled in the pit of her stomach as she got closer to her climax. So close, yet India held back, not wanting to come until her lovers did. She bit down hard on her bottom lip, catching her scream.

"Ah, fuck!" Rafe cried out as he shot his seed into her ass.

India couldn't hold back any longer as a violent jolt ripped through her entire body. Convulsing and shuddering, India rolled her eyes to the back of her head, and her breath came out in heavy gasps.

"Oh God, India!" Grant howled as he exploded within her.

They lay together, unmoving for several minutes, before Rafe slowly pulled out of her.

Grant rolled her to the side and India sighed and cuddled against them. Struck by the beauty of the moment, tears coursed down her cheeks.

Raising his head with alarm in his blue eyes, Grant asked, "Sweetheart? What's wrong?"

India sniffed. "I'm just so happy. I never thought I would ever be—that I didn't deserve it, but the two of you came into my life and now I don't know what I would do without you."

Grant gently stroked her cheek. "You are part of us now, India, just as we are a part of you."

Rafe kissed her shoulder. "We all deserve each other. You both mean so much to me that I can't do without either one of you in my life."

India smiled, the joy within her heart threatening to spill over. She kissed each man in turn. "I love you both so much, and there's no one else in the world I'd rather be stranded with."

Epilogue

Almost a year later, India couldn't believe how everything was falling into place. Just as Rafe predicted, people soon lost interest in their story, but not before Ellen's byline appeared in the newspaper about the special bond they shared. The article spoke of their trials and tribulations and told briefly of their past childhoods, but not going into too much detail.

In no way did the story make their special relationship sound sordid or dirty. Via the newspaper they received tons of letters. A few were negative, but most were positive. Some of the letter writers even shared their own experiences about being with more than one partner in a committed relationship.

The only real fallout from the news story was Rafe's ex-wife trying to make trouble. She made some harassing phone calls and had even begun showing up at their home. The men had to literally hold India back from killing the woman. They had to eventually take out a restraining order against her, which Angie violated, thinking the rules didn't apply to her. She was promptly arrested. It was the last they'd heard from her.

Then there was Trevor and Leila who threatened to sue India for the "lies" she'd told in the article about them. The message had been relayed through her aunt. India had laughed, not bothering to relay a message back to them. They didn't have a leg to stand on as there were plenty of witnesses who could attest to their treatment of her, Jack included.

A smile touched her lips when she thought of her brother. What a difference a year made. They kept in contact regularly. Trevor and Leila had disowned him when Jack had come out, but he didn't seem to mind. He'd moved to New York to take a job as an investment broker, something he seemed to like. Not only that, he was in a relationship and was happy. India got together with him once a month to have lunch. It was nice to finally be on friendly terms with her brother.

Rafe and Grant's business was flourishing, and after she'd passed the Pennsylvania State Bar, she found a job working as a public defender in the juvenile division for the city. The three of them were starting to talk about expanding their family of three to four and she couldn't wait.

India was so deliriously happy she sometimes had to pinch herself to make sure she wasn't dreaming.

She placed the photo of them they'd had taken on their vacation to Niagara Falls on the living room wall. Rafe and Grant came through the patio door. They'd been doing yard work and they looked hot and sweaty. Something about that sent a warm feeling to the pit of her stomach. Her desire for each of them had yet to fizzle out. Instead, it burned brighter than ever.

"Guess what? The last box is finally unpacked. We're now officially moved in." She grinned at them.

"And it only took us six months," Grant observed dryly.

"You can't blame me. Every time we would start unpacking you two found some way to distract me, and we'd end up in the bedroom. I can't help it if you guys are a couple of horndogs."

Rafe wiggled his eyebrows at her. "It's your fault for being so sexy we can't keep our hands off you."

India grinned. "The same can be said of you two. Speaking of which, I think this feat of finally unpacking deserves a celebration."

They walked toward her with slow deliberate movements and she knew exactly the type of celebration they had in mind.

Yes, things were definitely on the upswing and the best was yet to come.

About the Author

To learn more about Eve Vaughn, please visit www.evevaughn.com. Send an email to Eve at eve@evevaughn.com or join her Yahoo! group to join in the fun with other readers as well as Eve!

http://groups.yahoo.com/group/evevaughnsbooks

One woman's campaign to win the hearts of
the two men she loves.

Brazen
© 2007 Maya Banks

One year ago, Jasmine left Sweetwater Ranch and the Morgan brothers, no longer able to bear the painful dilemma of loving both men. She returns home with a new perspective and one goal. To make Seth and Zane Morgan hers.

Jaz may have left home an innocent girl, but she's returned a beautiful, sensual woman. Despite the attraction they've both felt for her for years, Seth and Zane aren't prepared for the full-on assault she launches on their emotions.

She wants them both, but Seth has no intention of sharing his woman. It's up to her to change his mind because she can't and won't choose between the two men she loves.

Available now in ebook and print from Samhain Publishing.

Enjoy the following excerpt from Brazen...

Jasmine rubbed her palms up and down her arms as she crossed the small courtyard by the pool and headed for the kitchen door. She was tired, bone-achingly so. Her ankle throbbed, and it had rained on her again on the way home.

Every light in the house was on, and the courtyard was cast in the glow from the dusk to dawn light. She trudged up to the kitchen door and paused. Her hand curled around the handle, and she took a deep breath.

The door opened soundlessly and she walked inside. Seth stood abruptly from the barstool he was perched on, and without a sound, he yanked up his cell phone and punched a number. He put the phone to his ear.

"Zane, she's home. She's fine."

He hung up and stared at Jasmine, his expression thunderous.

"Where the hell have you been?" he asked as he stalked over to her.

She didn't reply.

"You had us worried out of our minds. And Carmen. She's upstairs in tears. Is that any way to treat a woman who has been a mother to you?"

"A mother you'd take away from me," she said bitterly.

He looked startled.

She took a step forward and winced.

Seth cursed and swept her into his arms. He gripped her tightly as he strode toward the stairs. Every part of him was tense. There was no sense putting up a fight so she lay limply against him.

He paused outside Carmen's door. "Carmen," he shouted. "Jasmine's home. I'm taking her to her room. She's fine."

Carmen burst out of the door but paused when she caught Seth's scowl. Carefully she leaned forward, captured Jasmine's face in her hands and kissed her cheek. "Thank God you're safe, *niña*."

"I'm sorry, *mamacita*," she whispered back. "I never meant to worry you."

Carmen patted her cheek. "I know this, *niña*. You are a good girl. Now go, let Seth take care of you."

Jasmine looked sorrowfully at her as Seth started forward again, his abruptness with Carmen bordering on rude.

Once inside her bedroom, he put her down close to the wall. She stumbled back, and instead of steadying her, he pressed in close to her.

He ravaged her mouth, his lips working so hot, so intensely over hers. Her back met the hard surface of the wall, and she was trapped between it and Seth's body.

"You test every one of my limits," he rasped as his mouth worked down her jaw and to her neck. "I have no control when it comes to you."

"You don't want me here anymore," she said quietly.

He stopped, his lips pressed to the hollow of her neck. Then he slowly stood to his full height. His eyes looked haunted as he reached out to cup her cheek.

"I've always wanted you here, Jasmine."

"You said that I didn't belong here. That you...that Zane and Carmen weren't my family."

Tears glittered in her vision as she relived the devastation his words had caused.

Seth let out an agonized groan. He cupped her face in both

of his hands and lowered his head to hers. He kissed her long, gently, his lips tender against hers. He pulled away the barest of inches.

"I just want what's best for you, Jasmine. And sometimes...sometimes I worry that we've cheated you by sheltering you here for so long."

"What if it's what I want?" she whispered brokenly. "I don't want to leave here. I love you."

Seth pulled her closer until her face was buried in his chest. He laid his cheek on the top of her head and breathed in deep.

The door flew open, and Seth pushed her away almost guiltily. Jasmine turned to see Zane standing in the doorway, his expression relieved.

"Thank God, you're okay," he said.

Seth stiffened beside her and started to move away. "I'll leave you two alone," he said in a low voice.

"Don't go," she pleaded, knowing this was it. Do or die time.

He paused and looked at her with uncertainty written in his expression. "What are you asking, Jasmine?"

"Make love to me," she whispered. "Both of you. I need you both so much. You were wrong. This *is* where I belong. With you. Both of you."

There was calm acceptance on Zane's face. Seth's was a wreath of torture. He was torn, and she could see that despite his objections, despite all that he'd said, he wanted her. She moved forward, her intent to make it as easy on him as possible.

She melted into his arms. At first he didn't respond, but when she trembled and faltered on her bad ankle, he caught her against him.

"You don't know what you're asking me to do," he said hoarsely.

"I'm only asking you to love me," she said softly.

She reached up on tip toe to brush her mouth across his. As he pulled her to him, she turned her head to look at Zane. She pleaded silently for him to understand, to accept. All she could see was answering desire.

hot stuff

Discover Samhain!
THE HOTTEST NEW PUBLISHER ON THE PLANET

Romance, fantasy, mystery, thriller, mainstream and more—Samhain has more selection, hotter authors, and everything's available in both ebook and print.

Pick your favorite, sit back, and enjoy the ride! Hot stuff indeed.

SAMHAIN
PUBLISHING, LTD

WWW.SAMHAINPUBLISHING.COM

Printed in the United States
133978LV00004B/1-69/P